3⁰⁰

Lily the Rebel

Other Books Available

The Lily Series
  Here's Lily!
  Lily Robbins, M.D. (Medical Dabbler)
  Lily and the Creep
  Lily's Ultimate Party
  Ask Lily
  Lily the Rebel
  Lights, Action, Lily!
  Lily Rules!
  Rough & Rugged Lily
  Lily Speaks!
  Horse Crazy Lily
  Lily's Church Camp Adventure
  Lily's Passport to Paris
  Lily's in London?!

Nonfiction
  The Beauty Book
  The Body Book
  The Buddy Book
  The Best Bash Book
  The Blurry Rules Book
  The It's MY Life Book
  The Creativity Book
  The Uniquely Me Book
  The Year 'Round Holiday Book
  The Values & Virtues Book
  The Fun-Finder Book
  The Walk-the-Walk Book
  Dear Diary
  Girlz Want to Know
  NIV Young Women of Faith Bible
  Hey! This Is Me Journal
  Take It from Me

Lily the Rebel

Nancy Rue

Zonderkidz

We want to hear from you. Please send your comments about this book to us in care of the address below. Thank you.

Grand Rapids, MI 49530
www.zonderkidz.com

Zonderkidz.

The children's group of Zondervan

www.zonderkidz.com

Lily the Rebel
Copyright © 2001 by Women of Faith

Requests for information should be addressed to:
Zonderkidz, *Grand Rapids, Michigan 49530*
www.zonderkidz.com

ISBN: 0-310-23255-4

Published in association with the literary agency of Alive Communications, Inc., 7680 Goddard Street, Suite 200, Colorado Springs, CO 80920.

Interior design by Amy Langeler

Printed in the United States of America

04 05 06 07 08 09/❖ DC/ 15 14 13 12

So I say, 'Okay, we gotta get this done or Mr. Nutting's gonna give us all zeroes,' and Benjamin says, 'Who cares?' Then I say, 'I do! I've got an A in this class, and I wanna keep it,' and he's, like, 'Wow, big deal, man, an A—dude.' You know, he's acting all smart—and then the minute, I mean the *minute* Mr. Nutting looks over at us, Benjamin starts acting all perfect, like he's this little angel or something. I *so* wanted to gag. I mean, he's like, *so* fake. You oughta be glad he wasn't in your study group."

Lily took a breath and switched the phone to her left ear. On the other end of the line, her best friend Reni waited patiently. She knew, of course, that there was much more.

"Anyway," Lily went on, "I don't think kids who act all hypocritical like that deserve to be in accelerated classes. It's worse than if Shad Shifferdecker was in there."

"Uh, no," Reni said. "*Nothing* is worse than having Shad Shifferdecker in your class—especially a science class, with all those chemicals and stuff. What he couldn't do when Mr. Nutting's back was turned!"

"Shad doesn't bother me that much anymore, 'cause at least he admits that he thinks school is a total waste of time. What *bothers* me are boys like Benjamin who make the teachers think they're, like, these scholars, and then the rest of the time they get away with everything they can." Lily rearranged herself on the bed. "Oh—do you know what he did Monday when you weren't there?"

"No, tell me!"

"Okay—we're all taking this pop quiz, okay, and—"

"Lil—you're *still* on that phone?"

Lily stopped just short of propping her feet up on the wall and looked at her mom, who was standing in Lily's bedroom doorway with her gym bag in her hand.

Lily covered the mouthpiece with her hand. "I just got on," she said.

"Yeah—before I left for the gym—an hour and a half ago."

Only then did Lily notice that her mom's usually neat golden-brown ponytail was halfway out of its scrunchie and her cheeks were about the color of Pepto-Bismol.

"Oh," Lily said. "You already went?"

"Went. Worked out. Stopped at the gas station—the post office." Mom nodded toward the phone. "Your time's more than up. Say adios."

"Okay," Lily said, mane of red hair scattering as she nodded, "just let me finish telling Reni this one thing."

"I know your 'one things', Lil," Mom said. "Save it for the next marathon conversation."

"Do you need to make a call or something?" Lily said.

Mom squinted her doe-brown eyes a little—a sure sign that she was getting annoyed. "No," she said. "I just need for you to follow the rule. Thirty minutes."

"Art was on here for two hours last night!"

"Remind me to have him hanged at sunrise. Meanwhile—"

Mom made a cutting motion across her throat, and as she disappeared from the doorway, Lily sighed.

"I gotta go," she said into the phone.

"Did you go over time?" Reni said.

"Yeah. And I was just getting to the good part!"

"We can finish up tomorrow morning."

"You know what? When I get older and have my own place, I am *so* gonna talk as long as I want. I want one of those phones that—"

"Lilianna!"

"See ya," Reni said.

Lily hurriedly poked the off button on the portable phone. When Mom started calling her Lilianna, it was time to snap to. Lily rubbed at the prickly feeling, crawling up the back of her neck and looked down at her gray mutt, Otto, who was asleep on his back on the floor, all four paws in the air.

"If I had hackles like you," Lily said, "they'd be standing up right now."

She propped her long, lanky legs up on the wall and looked longingly at the phone.

I remember when I'd rather play word games with Dad than talk on the phone anytime, she thought. She ran her fingers over the receiver. *I used to wonder what people found to talk about for so long. Now I could yak to the Girlz all day and still not get it all in.*

"*There's* the phone. Dude, I've been looking all over for it."

Lily's brother Art sauntered into her room, blue eyes looking hungrily at the portable phone. He was tall and lean like Lily, but at sixteen, he had the whole lanky thing more under control. He snatched up the phone and flipped it deftly from one hand to the other, high over his short, red hair.

"The rule is you're supposed to put it back on the hall table when you're done," he said, "so the next person doesn't have to go looking for it."

"Then how come I had to dig under your bed for it when I wanted to use it?" Lily said.

"Otto musta dragged it under there. How ya doin', Muttsky?"

Otto lifted his wiry head and growled out of the side of his mouth. Art grinned.

"Thanks, Pal. I was starting to think you didn't love me anymore."

"Speaking of love," Lily said, nodding toward the phone, "are you gonna call Traci?"

"Traci? Nah, we broke up a long time ago."

"You just went out with her Friday night!"

"Oh. I guess time flies when you're having fun." He stopped juggling the receiver and narrowed his eyes at her. "Since when did you start keeping track of my love life?"

"Since you started hogging the phone all the time!"

"Like that makes a difference. We only get a half hour at a time anyway." His wide mouth went into a grin. "I just string my half hours all together."

"Get out," Lily said cheerfully.

He did, but her younger brother Joe appeared less than ten seconds later and tried to play the "Wipe Out" drum solo on the doorframe.

"What?" Lily said.

"Mom says to come down and set the table."

"It can't be my turn again!"

"It's right on the chart—U-G-L-Y. That's you, right?"

"Get out," Lily said—and this time not cheerfully.

"Don't do it, then," he said as he went off down the hall. "Get in trouble. See if I care."

Was I that obnoxious when I was nine? she wondered.

Once again she put her hand up to the prickly place on the back of her neck as she dragged herself down to the kitchen.

No, she thought, digging through the silverware drawer for at least two forks that matched. *When I was nine, I was all into putting on plays in the backyard and going through the trunks in the attic for dress-up stuff and wishing I was Jo in* Little Women.

The thought of it made her snicker. She had definitely changed. Now she was twelve—in the second month of seventh grade—spending most of her time doing homework and talking on the phone ... when she was allowed to.

"We need to put soup spoons on," Mom said. "Harriet sent me home with enough homemade vegetable soup for all of us." Her mouth twitched in that way that took the place of a smile. "None of us are going to get homemade soup any other way, that's for sure. I was hoping cooking would become one of your things, Lil. Then we might get some decent meals around here."

"What 'things'?" Lily said.

"Last month you were going to be the next Dear Abby. Last summer it was Martha Stewart. In May, you had—"

"Okay, I get it," Lily said. She dealt the plates onto the place mats, scowling. "They aren't 'things.' I was just trying to figure out what I wanted to do, that's all."

"Was?" Mom said. "Past tense?"

"Yeah."

"So you're, like, *so* over that?"

Her mouth was twitching at both corners, but Lily didn't find it the least bit amusing. She could feel the scowl getting deeper and the prickles getting pricklier.

"Could you please not make fun of the way I talk?" she said. "And that was just a phase I was going through. I know who I am now."

"I see."

"I'm *so* serious!"

Mom turned from the pot she was stirring on the stove and wiped her hands on the seat of her sweats. "I *so* know. Okay—sorry—no more teasing."

Good, Lily thought.

"Can I just ask you this, though?"

"Sure."

"Is it now safe to pack away your modeling portfolio, your first-aid kit—"

Lily didn't holler "Mo-om!" this time. She knew it was going to come out with an edge that would bring on the "Lily, don't take that tone with me." Instead, she said, through her teeth, "I'm going out to the laundry room to get some more napkins."

She found them right away, but she hiked herself up onto the top of the dryer and sat there for a few minutes, hugging the package of napkins to her chest. If she went back to the kitchen right now, she wasn't sure she could keep herself from hissing like a copperhead at everything Mom said.

This is so weird, she thought. *Just a couple of weeks ago, Mom and Dad were so cool. Now all of a sudden, it's like they're in my face all the time. It's driving me nuts!*

That, she knew, was why it was so much fun to talk to Reni and the other "Girlz"—Suzy, Zooey, and Kresha—on the phone.

Without them, Lily thought, *I'd go bonkers.*

"Where'd you go for those napkins, Lil?" Mom called from the kitchen. "Ireland?"

Lily sighed and slid off the dryer. She might just go bonkers anyway.

She thought about it some more that night when she was curled up with her Bible, her journal, China (her giant, stuffed Panda), and Otto. That was the usual setup for her quiet time with God.

"So, God," she wrote in her journal, "I know I'm supposed to get my mind all silent so I can hear you do that quiet-voice thing in there—but how am I supposed to get it to be still when everybody else is always *at* me?"

She closed her eyes and waited. Nothing came up except her hackles.

Then, God, could you please help me find a way to stop this prickling in my neck? It makes me act so cranky around here!

Home wasn't the only place where she wanted to tear out handfuls of her wild, red hair. Middle school, she decided the next morning, was enough to make her bald by the end of the semester.

That day, it started when she and the Girlz—except for Kresha—were gathered on their usual bench before first period, eating the Nutri-Grain bars Zooey had brought for all of them. They were being careful to put their wrappers in the trash can lest "Deputy Dog" pounce on them. She was the female, school cop who monitored the halls before and after school and between classes. Eighth graders said she went easy on people the first month of school, but right about now, she usually started writing people up right and left.

"What—no donuts?" Reni asked, as she peered into the grocery bag. "No cinnamon buns?"

"I don't eat that kind of stuff anymore," Zooey said. "Since I started losing all my baby fat from doing aerobics in PE, I figure why blimp back up again?"

"You were never fat," Suzy said. She tilted her head so that her silky-black bob of hair fanned across her cheek. "You were just . . . fluffy."

"Nah," Reni said, "she was fat—"

"Hey," Lily said quickly, "anybody know where Kresha is?"

"She had to go see her ESL teacher," Suzy said.

"Why?" Zooey asked, hazel eyes round. "She's doing great with her English now." Kresha was from Croatia and had recently experienced a learning spurt that was making her sound more American by the hour.

"Ask her," Reni said.

She nodded toward the stairs where a flush-faced Kresha was leaping down the "up" steps two at a time. Her wispy, sand-colored hair looked even more disheveled than usual, and her backpack was flying out behind her.

"Girl-za!" she shouted at them. "I have the good news!"

"And I have *bad* news."

All five heads turned to see Deputy Dog strolling out from under the staircase, thumbs hooked into her uniform belt. Her eyes were on Kresha, and as far as Lily could tell, she was practically licking her chops.

Kresha's excited grin didn't fade as she smacked her bangs away from her eyebrows and said, "I sorry. No yelling in the halls, right, sir?"

Reni grabbed on to Lily's arm, and Lily cringed. Zooey and Suzy looked as if they were both about to pass out.

Deputy Dog drew herself up out of her belt to full stature and glared at Kresha. "Contrary to popular belief," she said, "I am not a guy, so you can drop the sir."

Kresha shrugged happily and kept grinning as she edged toward the Girlz. "Okay," she said. "I never do it again."

"Excuse me?"

"I don't think she understood you," Suzy said to the officer. Her voice was jittery. Suzy seldom spoke up around adults, even when she *really* had to be excused to the restroom or something.

Deputy Dog looked at Suzy. "Was I talking to you, Missy?" she said.

Lily could see Suzy freezing right to the spot. Her face went so white that her dark eyes stood out like two buttons of fear. The prickles went up the back of Lily's neck.

"Was I?" the woman said.

Suzy shook her head.

"I can't hear your brains rattling in there. How about an answer?"

Leave her alone! Lily wanted to shout. *Can't you see she's scared to death?*

"No," Suzy said finally—in a voice frail as a spider web.

Deputy Dog looked as if she wanted to say more to Suzy, but Kresha raised her hand, as if she were in class.

Oh, no, Lily thought. *Kresha—not now!*

But Deputy Dog said, "I'll ask the questions. Put your hand down."

"I will not yell again," Kresha said. "I promise."

"Yeah, well, yelling's the least of your problems, Missy. Are you aware that you just came down the 'up' staircase—and at a dead run, no less?"

"It wasn't exactly a run," Reni muttered to Lily out of the side of her mouth.

"Do you know the rules in this school, Missy?" Deputy Dog said. "Or don't they print them in your language?"

"I know rules," Kresha said. Her eyes looked confused, but she was still smiling.

"Then am I to assume that you have no respect for them—like your friends here?"

The Girlz looked at each other, wide-eyed. Zooey, Lily saw, was close to tears, and Suzy was already sniffling.

"What did *we* do?" Reni said.

Deputy Dog reached behind Zooey's back and snatched away the grocery bag. "Eating in the halls," she said.

Lily cleared her throat. "Um—we didn't know we weren't supposed to eat. I don't think that's in the rules." She wanted to add, *Of course there's so many of them, who can remember them all?*

"We didn't throw our wrappers on the ground," Zooey said, voice teetering.

"Bully for you," Deputy Dog said. "I'll arrange for medals for all of you." She folded the top of the grocery bag and tossed the whole thing into the trash can. "No eating except in the cafeteria," she said. She pulled a pad out of her back pocket and a pencil from behind her ear. "Names," she said.

Suzy gave a full-out whimper, and Zooey let the floodgates go and started bawling. Deputy Dog drew up her mouth in disgust.

"Don't try that with me," she said. "I've seen enough tears to drown a litter of kittens, and it never works. Dry up and give me your names."

"Reni Johnson—"

"Kresha Regina—"

Lily put one arm around Zooey and one around Suzy, which left no hands for trying to smooth down the porcupine quills that were poking at her whole spine. *This is* so *not fair!* she wanted to scream. *Why don't you go find Shad Shifferdecker and haul him in—he must be doing* something *wrong—but leave* us *alone!*

"So are you going to tell me your name or are you planning to wait for your lawyer?"

Lily realized with a jerk that Deputy Dog was talking to her. The prickles turned inward and stabbed at her stomach.

"Lily Robbins," she said. "But—what's this for?"

"This little missy," she said, jabbing her chin toward Kresha, "is getting after-school detention for misbehaving in the halls. The rest of you are getting written warnings about food consumption in non-designated areas. Except you."

Her eyes—a muddy shade of brown—pierced into Lily's.

"Me?" Lily said.

"That's who I'm looking at. You are getting a referral to the counselor. The two of you need to talk about your bad attitude."

Chapter 2

The Girlz stood stone still as Deputy Dog scribbled on her pad of forms and tore each one off with a flourish. Lily was afraid to so much as swallow for fear her movement would get her something worse than a meeting with the counselor. On either side of her, she could feel Suzy and Zooey silently crying.

Reni, on the other hand, was far from tears. Lily could see her nostrils flaring as she fumed.

I know how you feel, Reni, Lily wanted to say. *This is* so *not right!*

When each of the Girlz had a citation in her hand, Deputy Dog gave them all one last muddy-eyed glare.

"This looks like a risky business to me, ladies," she barked, "the five of you hanging out here together. Kids will do things in a group they'd never dare do when they're alone. I suggest if you want to keep from getting into trouble, you stay away from each other before school."

She paused, as if she were waiting for them all to heartily agree, but nobody moved. If they were like Lily, they were all in shock.

Just as Deputy Dog looked as if she were going to have them sign a sworn statement to that effect, some other unsuspecting kid gave a yell from the other side of the staircase. Returning the pad to her back pocket with a snap, the school cop charged in his direction.

"I feel like warning him to run for his life," Reni whispered.

"How can you joke about it?" Zooey said, her voice thick with tears. "My mom is so gonna kill me."

"I don't know what to do," Suzy said. "I never got in trouble with the *police* before!"

"Me neither," Reni said.

Kresha didn't say anything. She just stared blankly at her citation.

"Do you get it, Kresha?" Lily said.

Kresha shook her head no.

"It means you have to stay after school for, like, an hour because you came down the wrong side of the stairs and you were running and yelling."

Kresha looked puzzled. "But—I have good news. When you have good news, you run and yell—up, down—no matter."

Reni grunted. "It matters to Deputy Dog. I'm surprised she didn't put you in handcuffs."

"Does she do that?" Zooey said, eyes nearly bulging from her head.

"You know what's the worst thing of all?"

The Girlz looked at Suzy. Her lower lip was trembling.

"What's the worst thing?" Zooey said. "I'm afraid to ask."

"That we can't meet before school anymore! With all the stuff that's going on with my parents and everything, I don't know if I can get through the day if I don't see all of you before first period!"

"I *so* don't think she can keep us from doing it," Reni said. "Can she Lily?"

Lily had the porcupine quills going up her spine again. "I'm gonna look in the rule book and see," she said. "And I'm gonna find out if 'bad attitude' is in there too."

"What is 'attitude'?" Kresha asked. "I want to know every English word—now I'm going to real classes."

"You *are*?" Zooey said.

"That is my good news," Kresha said. She tilted up her chin and grinned. "My ESL teacher say—no, *says*—I am ready for math and science in English."

The four of them all talked at once, chirping their congratulations until Lily shushed them, her eye wary for Deputy Dog.

"That is the coolest!" Reni said.

"What classes are you in?" Zooey said. Her face was beaming, all traces of tears long gone.

Kresha unfolded a piece of paper and read, "Math, third period—Mr. Chester. Science, seventh period—Mr. Nutting."

"That's our science class!" Suzy said. "Reni and Lily and me!"

"We'll all be together!" Lily said, and then she stopped.

Zooey's smile had crumpled into a line so forlorn that Lily wanted to bite her tongue off.

"I'm sorry, Zooey," she said. "But maybe next semester you can be with us."

"That's never gonna happen," Zooey said. "I'll never be as smart as all you guys."

"So maybe you could study really hard," Suzy said, "and show your teacher you need to be in the accelerated class, just like Kresha did."

Zooey snuffed up a noseful of tears. "Why do I have to change everything about myself? I worked so hard to lose all this weight so I could be skinny like you guys. Now I have to study every minute so I can be a genius too."

"We're not geniuses—"

The discussion continued around her, but Lily's thoughts were stirring too fast to latch on to any of it.

It's so stupid to divide people up into accelerated and regular and slow! We could help Zooey—we'd make sure she learned. Now she feels like she's dumb or something. Sometimes I hate this school!

Only when Suzy said, "Yikes, Lily," did Lily realize she'd said the last part out loud.

"Well, I'm sorry!" she said. "But this place is, like, so lame sometimes!"

"Yeah," Reni said. "And the *really* worst part is that we can't do anything about it."

"Right," Suzy said. She gave her puffy, tear-filled eyes one more rub and took Kresha by the hand. "Let's go before *she* comes back."

Suzy hurried off toward the locker area with Kresha in tow. Zooey followed them at a fast walk, glancing over her shoulders as she went. Reni looked up at Lily—she only came to Lily's shoulder—and her brown face looked even darker than usual.

"Do you think we should keep meeting here now?" she said.

"We don't have to meet *here*," Lily said. "I'll find us another place—someplace where she can't find us. I'm tired of people telling us how to live our lives!"

"Uh, Lily," Reni said, "we're, like, twelve. I think grown-ups are supposed to tell us how to live our lives."

"Not every stinkin' little thing! Otto has more freedom than I do!"

"Okay, but you better quiet down. She's liable to come back over here and write you up again."

"Let her," Lily said stubbornly. "Yeah, bring her on!"

Reni grinned as she grabbed on to Lily's backpack and pulled her toward the lockers. "You're out of control, girlfriend," she said.

That's just the point, Lily thought later during first-period music. They were supposed to be drawing their responses to Beethoven's "Fifth Symphony." So far, all Lily had down were a bunch of red and black scribbles.

I don't have control over anything. I might as well be two years old again!

She leaned back in her desk and looked at the window beside her. The October light was hitting it just right so that it formed a golden mirror on the glass. Lily stared at herself.

She didn't look two years old, she decided. Her red hair, though still thick and curly, wasn't quite as wild as it had been even a year ago, and most of her freckles had faded into clear, ivory-colored skin. She was even growing into her mouth, which until recently had seemed to her to resemble the Grand Canyon.

So if I can see how fast I'm growing up, she thought, *how come everybody treats me—and the Girlz too—like we're still in kindergarten?*

"Interesting drawing," said a voice behind her. "Can you give me some more?"

Lily barely glanced up at Ms. Bavetta, the music teacher. She didn't have to—they could probably smell her perfume all the way down in the gym.

"I'm still working on it," Lily said.

"Uh-huh. Where are you going with it?"

Lily studied her black-and-red scribbles again. "It's all about not having control," she said.

"I hear you," Ms. Bavetta said, and she moved on to the next desk.

Do you really *hear me?* Lily thought. *Does anybody?*

That was good for another couple of scribbles—in purple.

Later in the period, when Ms. Bavetta was calling people up to the front to talk about their drawings, Lily pretended to still be working on hers so she wouldn't have to be mortified by kids like Benjamin and Bernadette snickering at her in the back of the room. Just then an office aide came in.

"Lily," Ms. Bavetta said, "note for you."

"Busted!" Benjamin said.

"Class," Ms. Bavetta said, looking vaguely around. That was about the extent of her class discipline as far as Lily had been able to figure out.

Lily quickly unfolded the note, heart pounding. That Deputy Dog sure didn't waste any time—

But as her eyes caught the heading at the top—"From Mr. Miniver's Desk"—she sagged with relief. Mr. Miniver was the newspaper adviser, and he and Lily had become good friends during the short time she'd worked on the *Middle School Mirror* in September. A note from him was never about anything bad.

"Lily-Pad!" he'd written. "I hear you've run into a little trouble with the 'law.' Since I'm helping out the counseling staff until my new job starts, what do you say we chat second period during your study hall? I'll look forward to seeing your great smile!"

Lily could imagine his mustache turning upward as he made that last exclamation point.

She'd forgotten that Mr. Miniver was getting his master's degree and was going to be on the counseling staff in January instead of teaching journalism and English. So *he* was going to be the one talking to her about her "bad attitude," huh? She nervously peeled the paper off the purple crayon. Was this going to mean everything would be different between them now?

She made the biggest scribble yet across her drawing and managed to get through the period without having to explain it to the whole class. She was more than a little happy about that.

Benjamin made so much fun of Marcie McCleary's drawing of one of the Backstreet Boys, she crumpled it up in a ball and threw it at him, right across the classroom. Ms. Bavetta said, "Class—"

So Lily was glad when the bell rang, but she took her time getting to the counseling center. Even though she was seeing Mr. Miniver, she'd never been called to the office before, and it was scary.

Slim, blue-eyed Mr. Miniver, of course, didn't look scary at all as he opened the door to a conference room he was using for an office. He greeted her with a grin.

"Lily-Pad!" he said. "Good to see you!"

His eyes, as always, were warm and kind, and he talked in friendly exclamation points.

"We miss you on the newspaper," he said as he pulled a chair out for Lily.

"Oh, yeah. I'm sure Lance is crying himself to sleep every night."

"Lance-alot has some issues." Mr. Miniver sat down across the table from her and leaned on his elbows. "Why don't we talk about yours?"

"My issues?" Lily said. "I didn't even know I had any. It was Deputy Do—I mean, that police lady who said I had some. She said I had a 'bad attitude.' But I don't! I just thought she was being way unfair to Kresha, but I didn't, like, *say* anything!"

Mr. Miniver chuckled. "You seldom have to, Lily-Pad. Most of us can read your face like it was the *Burlington County Times*!"

"Oh," Lily said. She put her hand up to her cheek, but all she could tell about it now was that it was going blotchy.

"I wish you could see yourself in a mirror right now," he said. "I think your face is saying, 'If people can't understand me, I wish they'd just get out of my face.' How close am I?"

"Way close!" Lily said. "Only—I wasn't thinking that about *you*."

"Of course not!" He grinned and folded his slender fingers on the tabletop. "So—do you want to talk about who *is* in your face? Besides Deputy—uh, Officer Horn?"

Lily relaxed against the back of the chair. "It's almost this whole school, for openers. Every ten minutes I just want to scream at somebody, 'Stop being stupid!'"

"I have that urge myself from time to time."

"You do?"

"Sure. It's frustration. Very human. Especially at this time in your life. You're not a little girl anymore, but a lot of people treat you like one and they put so many limits on you, you're like a bag of popcorn in the microwave. You've watched one, haven't you?" he said, forming his hands into the shape. "It gets hotter and hotter and hotter until it just pops open!"

21

"I'm definitely about to pop open," Lily said.

"That's perfectly normal."

Lily fiddled with a curl for a minute. Mr. Miniver just waited. Finally, she said, "So Officer Horn wrote me up for being normal?"

"You're just as delightful as ever, Lily-Pad! I'm thinking I'm going to enjoy our little meetings."

"What little meetings?" Lily said. She could feel her eyes narrowing.

"You wouldn't mind coming in once or twice a week during second period to chat with me, would you?"

"I wouldn't mind," Lily said quickly. "But what would we talk about?"

"Being normal!" he said.

That kept her thoughts occupied the rest of the morning and on into lunch—that is, when she wasn't feeling "normal" about a dozen other things that happened.

They were studying subordinate clauses in English, and Mrs. Reinhold made them write the whole sentence in every one of the exercises in the unit. Lily liked Mrs. Reinhold, but she could be so old-fashioned, and what was the point?

In fourth-period geography, Ms. Ferringer drilled them almost the whole hour on the states and their capital cities, while Lily muttered to herself, "Why couldn't we just look it up if we wanted to know? Why do we have to memorize them?"

At lunch, the Girlz all sat together like they always did, which was fine until Suzy spotted Officer Horn surveying them from across the cafeteria.

"I want to tell her we're allowed to have food in *here*," Reni said.

"I wish you would," Zooey said. "She's creeping me out so bad I can hardly eat."

"I'd *love* to tell her," Lily said.

The other four suddenly looked as if they were squirming.

"What's wrong?" Lily said. "I'm not really gonna do it!"

"You sure looked like you were," Zooey said.

The prickles started up Lily's neck again and stayed there the rest of the afternoon—in fifth-period math when Mr. Chester gave a test and strolled up and down the aisles to make sure nobody was cheating, and in PE when the substitute teacher made them all take showers, even though their regular coach never did.

By the time Lily was on her way to science in seventh period, she felt like a pincushion. *One more prickle,* she thought, *and I'm going to explode!*

Then somebody stuck a "pin" in her.

Chapter 3

Science was her least favorite class. She'd always loved the experiments and stuff in elementary school, but her teacher this year was Mr. Nutting. It was pretty much unanimous among the students at Cedar Hills Middle School that he deserved the names the kids called him behind his back: Nut*case*, Nut*house*, Nut*bar*.

Lily herself didn't think he was exactly crazy. It was his talent for sarcasm that bothered her. And that day, it was fully operational.

"The bell has rung, people," he said. "Although *why* you would interpret that as a signal to be in your seats is anybody's guess."

"You're so witty, Mr. Nutting," Benjamin said. Beside him, Bernadette bobbed her head of curls.

That was the other thing that bugged Lily about this class: Mr. Nutting let kids like Benjamin and Bernadette and some of their "new in-crowd" friends to get away with having mouths as smart as his. And since they were trying to outdo the "old in-crowd"—people like Chelsea, Ashley, and Shad—they worked at it pretty hard. As far as Lily was concerned, none of it was terribly funny.

"Settle down," Mr. Nutting was saying now in his drone of a voice. He always sounded like he was bored with everything. "Take out your lab notebooks."

"Could I go to my locker and get mine?" Marcie said.

"Me too?" somebody else said.

Mr. Nutting played with his earlobe. "Is this just temporary insanity or a more permanent form of mental incapacitation?"

"Huh?" Marcie said.

"Dude, Mr. Nutting." Benjamin was wearing his I'm-so-impressed face. "Do you know, like, every word in the entire dictionary?"

Mr. Nutting didn't answer. He was looking at the door, which had just opened.

"It's Kresha!" Reni whispered to Lily.

"I hope he lets her sit over here," Suzy said.

"So what do we have here?" Mr. Nutting was saying. He took a pink slip from Kresha's hand. She was grinning at him, but he missed that as he frowned at the paper.

"Absolute geniuses they have down there in scheduling," he said. "It took them until the second month of school to discover you didn't have a science class. I hope you're bright, because you have a lot of catching up to do."

Kresha was still smiling as she watched his mouth.

"She doesn't understand half of what he's saying," Lily whispered to Reni.

"Kresha," Mr. Nutting said, still studying the pink slip like it was the Constitution. "So what do they call you?"

"Call me?" Kresha said. "Oh! 385–3108."

Both in-crowds roared. Benjamin accompanied them by pounding on his desk.

Mr. Nutting lazily waved them down. "O-kay," he said to Kresha. "I give it about three days. Why don't you find a seat?"

The Girlz waved frantically at her.

"There's no need to burn a fuse, ladies," Mr. Nutting said.

Kresha hurried toward them, still grinning happily, obviously unaware that the rest of the class thought they were watching The Three Stooges. Lily's neck was one big prickle.

I think my popcorn bag's about to explode, she thought. *If he makes fun of Kresha one more time—I might just go* normal!

While everybody was dragging their lab notebooks out from various places and gathering at the counter where Mr. Nutting did his demonstrations, Suzy, Reni, and Lily rallied around Kresha and got her sorted out.

"Don't take everything he says seriously," Reni said to her.

"Just do the work and don't ever raise your hand," Suzy said. "That's what I do."

"He oughta be nicer," Lily said.

Reni shook her head. "Yeah, well, he's not, and there's nothing we can do about it."

"He is nice!" Kresha said.

Lily figured Kresha was in love with the whole world as long as she got to be in their class. Lily narrowed her eyes at Mr. Nutting. He just better not hurt Kresha's feelings.

Mr. Nutting finally got the class settled down and picked up a container filled with a clear liquid.

"Who remembers what this is called?"

"Water," Benjamin said.

"Very funny, Clyde." Mr. Nutting called all the boys Clyde.

"H–2–O?" Marcie said.

"R–2–D–2?" Bernadette said.

"Knock it off, clowns." Mr. Nutting tapped on the glass container. "I'm talking about this thing."

Lily raised her hand.

"Yeah, Red?"

"A beaker," Lily said through gritted teeth.

"Correct," he said, with his own teeth clamped together. "You oughta do something about that jaw problem, Red."

It's Lily! she wanted to scream. But he'd already moved on.

"I'm going to pour the contents of this—" He paused and gritted his teeth. "Beaker—into one of these, which is called a—"

"Glass cigar," Benjamin said.

Mr. Nutting made a loud buzzing noise. "No! Thanks for playing. Who else?"

"Test tube!" Marcie said.

"Congratulations. You do have a brain. Yes, now in the bottom of this test tube is a substance that will not react with water. We don't know what is in this—" He held up the beaker—and he looked at Kresha. "What did we say this was, Crusha?"

Kresha! Lily nearly shrieked. She was gritting her teeth so hard, they were starting to ache.

Kresha tilted her chin proudly. "Speaker!" she said.

"Speaker!" Mr. Nutting said. "What's the matter, Crusha, forget those Q-Tips today?"

"What is Q-Tip?" Kresha said, her smile fading only slightly. "That vord I do not know."

"Wonderful," Mr. Nutting said. "Go directly from ESL to accelerated science. Do not pass go. Do not collect $200. Let's all play Education Monopoly!"

"She can't help it if she was born in another country! She's still smart—smarter than probably anybody in here! Why don't you just leave her alone?"

It wasn't until Reni said, "Chill out, Lil," under her breath that Lily realized the outburst had come from her own lips. The look on Mr. Nutting's face confirmed it.

There was a long blur, and Lily was once more sitting in the office. Nobody said anything to her except "Sit there," which she did until the last bell rang. Then Mr. Miniver appeared and squatted beside her, and the blur cleared.

"Well, Lily-Pad," he said. "I said we'd talk again, but I had no idea it was going to be this soon. You want to come in and tell me what happened?"

When Lily stood up to follow him into the conference room, she saw four faces crowded into the office doorway. Every one of them clearly said, *Lily—we're so scared for you!*

"Ladies, this is not a sideshow," the secretary told them. "Unless you have business in here, you need to move on."

They peeled themselves away, and Mr. Miniver nodded toward the conference room. His eyes were still kind, and Lily took a deep breath. When he asked her to tell him the story, she poured it out without so much as a pause. Mr. Miniver followed it all with his liquid-blue eyes.

When she wound up with her final tirade at Mr. Nutting, Mr. Miniver glanced down at the sheet he was holding. Lily recognized it as the referral Mr. Nutting had written before sending her to the office.

"As usual, you're completely honest, Lily-Pad," Mr. Miniver said. "He quotes on here exactly what you just told me." He tugged at his mustache before he looked at her again. "That was quite an outburst."

"I was so mad! He didn't have any right to make fun of Kresha like that. She doesn't deserve to be put down just because she doesn't speak English that well yet!"

"I understand what you're saying. I just wish you'd saved it for our next session and vented to me instead of to him."

Lily blinked. "But you said it was normal for me to get mad when stuff like this happens! You said you do it yourself sometimes!"

Mr. Miniver put up a slender finger. "I said it was normal to *feel* that way. I didn't say I lashed out at people in situations where it isn't appropriate." He let one side of the mustache go up. "If I'd known you were going to go out and field test what I said right away, I'd have told you this sooner!"

"So it's normal that I *feel* mad, but I'm not supposed to do anything about it?" Lily's prickles were nearly out of control. "That makes me even madder!"

"I didn't say you couldn't do anything about it. I'm just suggesting that some of the things you might do are not appropriate—like yelling at your teacher. Do you pop off at your parents like that?"

"Are you kidding? I'd be grounded for life. *Longer* than life."

"So you need to think of your teachers the same way—they're people you need to treat with respect even though, I'll grant you, they don't always earn it."

Lily looked at him closely. "Do *you* think Mr. Nutting was being fair to Kresha?"

"What I think isn't the point. This is about you dealing with the feelings you have in a way that keeps you from being sent to the office every other period."

"I guess I don't know how to do that," Lily said. Her head felt suddenly heavy, and she wanted to bury it in her arms on the table until it all went away—or she turned eighteen—whichever came first.

"That's why they pay me the big bucks, Lily-Pad," Mr. Miniver said. "I'm going to help you figure out how. And knowing you, I bet a lot of good is going to come out of this. You could be a real advocate for minority kids like Kresha."

"What's an advocate? And please don't tell me to go look it up. That's what my dad always does."

"Which is probably why you're so wonderfully verbal," he said, grinning. "An advocate is a person who pleads someone else's cause, you know, kind of supports them in seeing that their rights aren't violated."

"Oh," Lily said. For the first time in hours, the porcupine quills going up her spine smoothed out, and suddenly there was room in her mind for something besides angry thoughts. "So how do I get to be one of those advocate people?" she said.

"That's something we can talk about in our sessions, which I'm thinking we need to have three times a week during your study hall. Can you handle that?"

"Sure. I never have anything to do in there anyway. I do all my homework the night before—" Her voice trailed off as a new vision took over—Lily Robbins, student advocate, smiling modestly with her arm around a glowing Kresha while a throng of middle-school students cheered them on. How she was going to *get* to that place, she had no idea—but the end result looked pretty good in her mind.

Maybe I should start watching more news shows, she thought. *And reading biographies of famous advocates, like—well, like somebody. Dad will know. I'm gonna have to start a binder for all my stuff—no maybe some files—okay, what about a whole filing cabinet?*

"So—you just give this to your study-hall teacher tomorrow and then come on down," Mr. Miniver was saying. He held out a yellow slip of paper. "And promise me you won't do anything drastic until then, okay?"

"Okay. Oh—but what about Mr. Nutting? Is he gonna give me a zero for today?"

"That's his call. I'll talk to him."

"You'll be my advocate!"

"Atta girl! I'm always on your side, Lily-Pad. You remember that, okay?"

"Okay!" Lily said. And she sailed out of the office, head full of ideas. *I feel* free! she thought. *This is so cool!*

She hoped the Girlz were still around. She couldn't wait to tell them—and they'd want to help, of course. The five of them always did stuff together—and wouldn't Reni be good at it? She wasn't afraid to speak up, once you got her going. And Kresha too. Zooey and Suzy might take some work, but they could do the behind-the-scenes things. This was big stuff. You didn't put a word like "advocate" on something that wasn't important.

Lily went to her locker, looking around for the Girlz as she sorted out what to take home. There was no sign of them, but maybe they'd be on the bench waiting for her.

No, she told herself. *They're too scared of Deputy Dog. Maybe that could be my first project as an advocate—getting our place back!*

She slammed the locker door and turned around. Two people blocked her way—but it wasn't Reni, Zooey, Suzy, or Kresha. It was Bernadette and Benjamin.

"We want to talk to you," Bernadette said.

"Yeah." Benjamin looked at her with his hard brown eyes. "It's about what happened in Mr. Nutting's class."

Chapter 4

Lily tried not to look as nervous as she suddenly felt. She licked her lips casually and looked them both in the eye. "So what's up?" she said.

"You totally went off on Nuthouse," Benjamin said.

"Yeah, well, he was picking on Kresha. She's my friend."

"But you weren't even, like, scared of him or anything," Bernadette said.

Lily couldn't help grunting. "You two aren't scared of him either. You talk back to him all the time."

"But not like that." Bernadette shook her curling-iron curls. "We pretend like we're kidding when we do it."

"You're not?" Lily said.

Benjamin let his lower lip sag. "Uh, no-o. I'm being totally sarcastic when I say stuff to him. He just doesn't know it."

Bernadette was nodding. "We *want* to say stuff like you said to him today—only we don't because we'd get in so much trouble."

"What'd they do to you, by the way?" Benjamin said.

"I just have to go to counseling," Lily said.

"Dude—you got a break. They'd put me in detention for the whole rest of the semester if I yelled at a teacher like you did."

"*See*, that's the thing." Bernadette was really in earnest now. She was forgetting to toss her hair around. "You can say stuff like that and get away with it because you never do anything wrong—"

"Plus, you know a lot of big words."

"My dad's a professor," Lily said. She knew it sounded lame, but she needed to stall for time while she figured out what was going on here.

"Okay," Benjamin said. "So we were thinking you could help us."

"With what?" Lily said.

Bernadette leaned forward and got so close to Lily's face, Lily could smell her chewing gum. If Deputy Dog caught her with *that*, Bernadette was definitely going down.

"Listen," Bernadette said. "You know Ms. Bavetta—first period?"

"Yeah—what about her?"

"All this year she's been letting us sit wherever we want to in her class. Then all of a sudden, after class today, she tells me and Benjamin that we can't sit together anymore."

"She says we're talking too much and disturbing the class," Benjamin said. "Yeah, right, like the whole thing isn't already disturbed."

"She isn't the best disciplinarian in the world," Lily said.

Benjamin and Bernadette looked at each other. "I told you she knew all the big words," he said. "She's gonna be great."

"At what?" Lily said. "What do you want me to do?"

"Convince Ms. Bavetta to let us keep sitting wherever we want to," Bernadette said. "It isn't fair for her to start out running the class one way and then suddenly change."

"Besides that, we aren't the only ones 'disturbing the class.'" Benjamin started ticking off on his fingers. "There's that Ashley chick, and her friend—Shirley or something—"

"Chelsea—"

"Plus Marcie McCleary, who *never* shuts her mouth."

"So, you just want me to talk to Ms. Bavetta for you?" Lily said.

"No—we want you to get in her face like you did Nuthouse," Benjamin said. "You know she won't send you to the office."

"Right," Bernadette put in. "She thinks you're so 'interesting.' Which you are," she added quickly, "but in a cool way, you know."

"I don't think I can just go in there and start yelling," Lily said. "I was mad at Mr. Nutting. It's not like I can make myself feel something."

"Wow," Bernadette said, "you're so deep."

"That's why you gotta do this," Benjamin said. "And what if she moves you away from *your* friends? She could, you know. Who knows—we could go in there tomorrow and find out there's a whole new seating chart, like Mrs. Reinhold!"

That would be a drag, Lily had to admit. Being an advocate wasn't about doing stuff for yourself—it was about standing up for other people who were having unfair things done to them. Besides, this was the first time Benjamin had ever said a nice word to Lily.

Maybe if he wasn't being treated so unfairly, she thought, *he wouldn't be such a jerk all the time.*

She looked at the two of them again. Bernadette was practically begging with her eyes, and Benjamin had his fingers crossed.

"How do I know it'll even work?" Lily said.

"Are you kidding?" Benjamin said. "If it worked on Nuthouse, it'll work on anybody."

Bernadette grabbed Lily's hands. "You should have seen how he changed toward your friend, Crush-Up or whatever her name is, after you left."

"Yeah," Benjamin said, "he just sent you to the office so we'd all know he was still the big boss and all that, but he was, like, way nicer to her because you gave him grief."

"Really?" Lily said.

"Totally."

"He was like a whole other person."

Now, *that* was a different story. *Maybe I really* am *supposed to be an advocate,* Lily thought. *Maybe this is even God telling me to do it! I'm supposed to listen to his voice, right?*

Benjamin and Bernadette were still watching her intently.

"Okay," Lily said. "I'll be your advocate."

"Yes!" Benjamin said.

"When are you gonna do it, Lily?" Bernadette said. "Tomorrow?"

"I don't know, " Lily said. "I have to formulate a plan."

"Wow," Benjamin said. "You are so smart."

Lily got started right away. As soon as she got home, she sprawled out on the family room floor with the remote and watched Judge Judy on TV. She kept a pad of paper next to her and jotted down tips: Don't take any nonsense off of people. . . . If they're talking stupid, cut them off. . . . Be fair, even if you have to rule in favor of some slimeball.

Lily chewed on her eraser and considered that last one. Bernadette and Benjamin weren't exactly slimeballs—not like Ashley and Chelsea who were out-and-out mean to people. But she had never particularly *liked* B&B either. There was something about them—besides the fact that they had a tight little group that thought they were totally cool—something that bothered Lily. She couldn't quite put her finger on it.

But they're right, it doesn't seem fair for Ms. Bavetta to pick on only them when everybody in that class is out of control. She glanced at the stern-looking woman in the black robe on the TV screen. *I need to be like Judge Judy and just fight for what's right, no matter who I have to defend.*

"All right, all hands on deck!"

Lily peeled her eyes from the screen. It was Mom, using her coach-voice. She was a PE teacher at the high school and coached the girls' volleyball team. When she went into that mode, it meant work.

"Let's go—Joe—Art—Lily! Front and center!"

"I did all my chores!" Lily called out to her.

"This isn't a chore. Come on—hop to it."

Feeling only slightly prickly in the neck, Lily snapped off the remote and went into the kitchen. Mom was standing there with three rakes in her hands.

"Looks like chores to me," Joe said.

Lily nodded. For once the absurd little creep had a point.

"Don't think of it as a chore," Mom said as she handed out the rakes to them. "Think of it as family time."

"Oh, yeah," Art said, grinning. "We're gonna bond while we rake leaves."

"No, the bonding comes later," Mom said. "If we can get the whole yard raked and the leaves bagged by Saturday night, we can all go to the game."

"Uh, Mom," Art said. "I got a news flash for you: I play in the band. I go to every football game anyway."

"Silly me. How *could* I have missed that?" Mom pushed open the back screen door and waved them out. "I thought you might be a little bored with high school football. Your Dad and I thought you'd like a change of pace."

"Not his college team, Mom," Joe said as he backed down the steps with his rake. "They're just a bunch of smart people. Their team stinks."

"Yes, we've smelled it," Mom said. "Which is why we're taking you to an Eagles game. Sunday. In Philly."

Joe shouted, "Yes!" and took a tumble down the last two steps. Art picked Mom up and set her out of the way. "Excuse me, ma'am," he said. "I got rakin' to do."

Mom's mouth was twitching double-time. She looked at Lily. "I know this isn't a thrill for you, but I thought you'd have fun watching the cheerleaders and the halftime show. You never see those things on TV. If all else fails, they have great hot dogs." She touched Lily gently under the chin. "It'll be good to do something as a family. I told you, I'm not going to be so focused on my job anymore. I want to spend more time with you kids."

Her eyes were so shiny, and she was almost smiling. Lily didn't have the heart to say, *But a* football *game?* After all, she remembered, she was the one who had told Mom just a few weeks ago that she wanted to spend more time with her.

But that was a few weeks ago, Lily thought. With a sigh, she dragged her rake to the far corner of the backyard. *I've got other stuff to think about now.*

Which brought her back to the problem of Ms. Bavetta. Lily raked and thought and raked and imagined and raked and planned.

It did occur to her after about the fifth bushel she dumped into Dad's wheelbarrow that Mr. Miniver had told her not to do anything drastic until she talked to him. But this wasn't drastic. She wasn't going to yell or lose control. That, she decided, was just the point. It was all going to be perfectly controlled. The question was, how? The harder she thought, the harder she raked.

"What's this, your eighth load?" Dad said when she dumped yet another bushel into the wheelbarrow. "I didn't know you were that into football."

"I'm not," Lily said. "I'm into *advocates.* Do you know any?"

Dad set the wheelbarrow back down on all fours and looked thoughtfully up at the waning afternoon sun. "The first two that come to mind are Martin Luther King Jr. and Gandhi. Both of them were effective advocates for the downtrodden. They used that whole passive resistance thing. Do you know about that?"

Lily shook her head.

"King learned it from Gandhi, I think. Anyway, the basic idea is that instead of fighting back with violence when they are discriminated against, people should just refuse to move from a place where they have every right to be until somebody moves them by force, and even then, they should go peacefully."

"I don't get it," Lily said.

"Okay—before the Civil Rights Amendment, the African-Americans got a pretty raw deal down South. They were told they had to sit in the back of the bus, for instance. So one day a woman by the name of Rosa Parks sat in a seat near the front. The bus driver told her to move to the back, but she just sat there. She didn't yell at him or swear at him or anything. She just stayed put. It was the beginning of a movement to ensure that African-Americans were given the same freedoms as other citizens."

"So if this was back then," Lily said, "Reni wouldn't get to sit next to me on the school bus."

"No," Dad said. He smiled faintly. "You and Reni probably wouldn't even know each other because you wouldn't go to the same school. There were separate schools for whites and blacks—"colored," as they used to call them."

"Nuh-uh!"

"Oh, yeah. If you and Reni went into a restaurant together, they'd serve you, but not her."

Lily put her hands on her hips. "There is no way I would ever let somebody treat Reni that way! I'm glad we don't live back then."

"Unfortunately, there are still people who think African-Americans are inferior. They wish we'd go back to the old 'rules'—which, by the way, were never written down. Everybody just followed them because that's the way it was done."

"I wouldn't," Lily said.

"So are you two going to *rake* these leaves, or just *talk* about them?" Mom said. She put her arms around Dad from behind and twitched her mouth up at him.

"We're busted, Liliputian," Dad said. "We better get back to work."

But Lily was already back to work—right there in her mind, where her plan for Ms. Bavetta was slowly changing.

Chapter 5

"You're gonna do *what?*" Reni said to her the next morning.

"Aren't you gonna get in trouble for that, Lily?" Suzy said.

Zooey was nodding, eyes round. "You already got in trouble yesterday—*twice!*"

"And we could get in trouble again today," Suzy put in. She glanced down the bleachers. "Are you sure it's okay for us to meet up here?"

Lily looked around the gymnasium. "This is the best place I could come up with on short notice."

"Does Deputy Dog come in here?" Zooey said nervously.

"What if Ms. Bavetta turns you over to *her* after you do this thing first period?" Suzy said—even more nervously than Zooey.

Lily folded her arms across her chest. "Don't you guys care about seeing justice done?"

"Sure," Reni said. "But what's that got to do with Benjamin and Bernadette wanting to sit together so they can go ga-ga over each other?"

"It's about things being fair," Lily said with exaggerated patience. "What if Ms. Ferringer separated *us*—or Mr. Chester? How would *we* feel?"

Reni's dimples got deeper as she considered that. "I did hate it when Mrs. Reinhold wouldn't let us sit together."

"I hate it that I can't even be in the same classroom as any of you guys!" Zooey said.

"See?" Lily said. "You need an *advocate*. If this works, then I can start on bigger stuff."

Suzy drew her tiny black brows together. "I don't know, Lily. This just sounds like trouble to me."

"The trouble isn't with me, though," Lily said. "It's with society. I read it in the encyclopedia last night—the part about Martin Luther King."

"The guy that started the Protestant thing?" Zooey said.

"No!" Reni rolled her eyes. "That was Martin Luther. This is a whole other person."

Zooey sighed. "I'm never gonna get as smart as you guys."

"Yes, Zo-wee!" It was the first time Kresha had said anything all morning, and they all looked at her now. She was leaning against the wall on the top row of the bleachers, an unusually sober look on her face. Lily had always suspected that the reason Kresha smiled constantly was because she didn't know what people were talking about half the time. Right now, her straight line of a mouth showed she understood stuff just fine.

"You are smart, Zo-wee," Kresha said. "These teachers—they are the ones who are—what is vord?"

"Stupid?" Reni said.

"But don't say that to their faces," Suzy said quickly. Her eyebrows were looking more worried by the minute.

"That's right, Kresha," Lily said. "I'm an *advocate* so I know what I'm doing—sort of—but we shouldn't go around yelling at teachers and telling them exactly what we think of them. There are better ways, which I'm learning more about all the time." She glanced at her watch.

"In fact, I have to go to the library right now and get some books on Gandhi."

"Are you *sure* you want to do this?" Reni said. "It's kinda freakin' me out."

Lily got a more positive reaction from Benjamin and Bernadette when she gave them their instructions right before first period.

"This is awesome!" Benjamin said.

"All we have to do is sit there?" Bernadette said.

Lily nodded. "I'll do the rest."

"This is gonna be *rad*," Benjamin said. "Come on, 'Dette."

Lily hurried to her own seat and watched as Benjamin and Bernadette took their usual places in the back, side-by-side. As always, Bernadette scooted her desk over closer to Benjamin's so it was out of line with the others in her row. Then they crossed their arms over their chests and waited.

So far, so good, Lily thought.

The bell rang, and the other kids wandered to their seats. Ms. Bavetta wasn't big on everybody being in place right at the start of class—which was why she didn't appear to notice Bernadette and Benjamin until she got to Bernadette's name on the roll.

"Oh," she said. "Bernadette? Don't you remember our little chat after class yesterday? You and Benjamin both need to move."

"No, ma'am," Bernadette said. Her voice was even and respectful, just the way Lily had coached her. "This is my seat."

Ms. Bavetta fiddled with her necklace. "It *was* your seat. Now you'll need to choose a new one. Let's see—Marcie, would you please trade places with Bernadette?"

But before Marcie could even stand up, Bernadette said, "No, ma'am. This is my seat."

"I don't have time for this," Ms. Bavetta said. "Benjamin—you move. I'll deal with Bernadette later."

41

Slowly Benjamin shook his head. Lily could tell he was enjoying himself.

"No, I'm not going to move either," he said calmly. "This is my seat."

By now the class was stirring with an undercurrent of excitement. Lily felt a little electrified herself.

"This is not a sit-in, boys and girls," Ms. Bavetta said.

"What's a sit-in?" Marcie said.

Ms. Bavetta ignored her. "Benjamin. Bernadette. Enough games. Come on, both of you. Get up and move elsewhere."

Neither of them did, although Benjamin cut his eyes over at Lily. It was time.

Lily raised her hand. "Ms. Bavetta?" she said.

Ms. Bavetta glanced at her, irritation etched on her face. "What is it, Lily?"

"I think Benjamin and Bernadette are right—those *are* their seats. At least they have been all year. It doesn't seem like it's fair for you to change the rules all of a sudden."

"They've been taking advantage of the freedom I've given them and the others in the class," Ms. Bavetta answered. "You abuse your rights—they get taken away."

"They're not the only ones, though," Lily said. "If you're going to move them—you ought to move everybody."

That brought on a chorus of protests from every corner.

"Class—" Ms. Bavetta said.

Nobody listened.

"Cla—a—a—ss!"

It got about one decibel quieter.

"All right!" Ms. Bavetta said. "I have neither the time nor the desire to rearrange the whole room. Benjamin, if you and Bernadette behave yourselves, you can stay there. I don't care—as long as I can get on with class?"

It sounded like a question. Lily raised her hand again.

"*What*, Lily?" Ms. Bavetta snapped.

"I think everybody's gonna be a lot happier now."

"That's interesting," Ms. Bavetta said dryly, "since absolutely nothing has changed."

As she turned to put on a CD, Lily glanced back at Benjamin and Bernadette. Ben gave Lily a thumbs-up sign. They certainly looked happy—and Lily herself had never felt smugger.

Yep, she decided, *I'm gonna like being an advocate.*

She couldn't wait for her meeting with Mr. Miniver so she could fill him in, and she was hurrying out of the room at the end of first period when somebody grabbed her arm. It was Benjamin.

He dragged her out into the hall with Bernadette hot on his heels.

"That was awesome!" he said when they were out of Ms. Bavetta's earshot.

"I thought for a minute she was going to make *everybody* change seats," Bernadette said, "and I was like, 'Whoa, Lily, what's up with that?'"

"But then you pulled it off!" Benjamin stuck out his hand.

Lily looked at it for a few seconds before she realized he wanted her to shake it. She did.

"You know what really gets me?" Bernadette said.

Lily shook her head.

"You don't *look* like the rebel type."

"That's 'cause I'm not."

"Yeah, but see, you *are*," Benjamin said. "You're taking on *teachers*."

"Yeah, you look like Anne of Green Gables or somebody, you know, all sweet and dressed by the rules," Bernadette said. "Nobody would ever think you were a—what was that thing you said?"

"Advocate?" Lily said.

"Yeah—to look at you, nobody would know. They'd think you were teacher's pet or something."

"The bell's gonna ring," Benjamin said.

Bernadette gave Lily one more grateful look. "Thank you *so* much. You're, like, the best."

But Lily barely heard her. As she hurried down the hall, she was already trying to imagine what an *advocate* looked like.

Mr. Miniver met her in the conference room and twinkled his eyes at her.

"I see you have a smile today," he said. "That's nice to see."

"I'm happy," Lily said. "I was just an advocate for somebody—and it worked!"

"Oh?"

"I didn't do anything drastic," Lily said quickly. "I hardly had to do anything at all—that was the beauty of it."

"You see?" Mr. Miniver said. "I knew you were going to be a quick study. You want to hear what Mr. Nutting said?"

"Is it bad?"

"No."

"Then yes, I do."

"He said he was probably a little out of line so he could see why you blew up, but that didn't excuse you for doing it in front of the whole class." Mr. Miniver nodded at Lily. "We talked about that yesterday."

"Right."

"So he said as long as you and I were working it out, you could come back to class, no hard feelings. You can get the notes on the demonstration from one of your friends."

"Thank you," Lily said. Her hands were sweaty with relief.

"There's one thing he did seem concerned about, though, Lily-Pad. He said that in the last couple of weeks, your attitude has been changing. Where have we heard that word before?"

"Depu—Officer Horn." Lily let out an exasperated puff of air. "But I don't get what they're talking about."

"Attitude is easy to see in other people—not so easy to see in yourself. I think what we have to do is look for what's going on inside you that you aren't even seeing."

"Are you still going to teach me how to be an advocate?"

Mr. Miniver's mustache did its little dance. "You are a character, Lily-Pad! I don't think I have to do much teaching—I think it's in your blood."

"Like Martin Luther King—or Gandhi?"

"Could be. The important thing is for you to know who you are and what you're feeling so you'll be able to choose those things that are worth standing up for. Otherwise, you'll be protesting that there aren't any Diet Dr. Peppers in the soda machines—things like that." He folded his hands on the tabletop. "So, shall we take a look at Lily?"

"Sure," Lily said.

But as Mr. Miniver asked her a bunch of questions and she answered them, Lily's mind was only half there. The other half was focused on something else he'd said—about choosing causes that were worth standing up for.

From now on, I'm only going to fight for worthy causes, she decided. *And I'm going to use passive resistance. And I'm going to start looking like an advocate.*

She was still thinking about it when she got to third-period English. Thankfully, she was paying enough attention to hear Mrs. Reinhold saying, "Your next book report must be on a biography. I want to know your choice by Monday."

As soon as Mrs. Reinhold gave the day's reading assignment and went back to her desk, Lily went up to her, book in hand.

"Can—may I do my book report on Gandhi?" she said. She held out the library book. "I just got this today."

Mrs. Reinhold peered through the lenses of her tiny glasses and gave a nod. "Good choice, Lilianna," she said. "I think you'll learn a great deal from that."

You don't even know! Lily thought as she headed back to her seat. Then she hurried through the class assignment so she could get started on Gandhi.

"Did you know he refused to *eat* for, like, weeks at a time?" she said to the Girlz at lunch.

Kresha hungrily eyed the piece of pepperoni pizza she was about to bite into. "I could not do that," she said.

"This guy looks like a freak," Zooey said. She looked up from the cover of Lily's book. "Why did he shave his head and wear a diaper?"

"I haven't gotten that far," Lily said. She secretly hoped that wasn't part of being an advocate. She didn't think she'd look especially good with a bald head and Pampers.

"Tell me again why you're reading that," Reni said.

"So we can learn how to be *advocates.*"

Suzy stopped with her fork halfway to her mouth. "We?" she said.

"Yeah," Lily said. "I've been thinking about it, and it just seems to me that we—you know, the Girlz Only Club—should be doing something important, you know, like standing up for the downtrodden."

"What is that vord—'downtrodden'?" Kresha asked.

"People like you," Lily said. "You know—you get discriminated against—or like Reni. Some people still think African-Americans are inferior."

"But I don't know anyone who thinks I'm inferior," Reni said. "I make all A's in accelerated classes. Mr. Lamb says I'm practically a shoo-in for All-State Orchestra—which reminds me, I have to practice after school, so I'm gonna be a little late for Girlz Club."

"We'll save some snacks for ya," Zooey said. "My mom's making them for us today—oh, and wait 'til you see the basement. She's got it all set up for us—it's so cool!"

"Okay," Lily said. "We'll talk about being advocates then. Meanwhile, be looking for a good cause." She looked at Kresha. "Things that make you mad—understand?"

"Yes," Kresha said. Her face broke into her usual grin. "But I am never mad!"

"Yeah, well, stick around here long enough and you will be," Lily said. "Everyone be on the lookout."

As it turned out, Lily didn't have to look very hard, or for terribly long, to spot her next project. She had to leave Mr. Chester's class on a hall pass to go to the restroom, and as she was hurrying back, somebody behind her called out, "Robbins, I want to see you."

Lily had the urge to come to attention and salute. Instead, she quickly turned around. It was Deputy Dog.

"I have a hall pass," Lily said, waving the blue slip in the air.

"Put it away, Robbins. I'm not here to bust you. I want to pay you a compliment."

"Oh," was all Lily could say.

"I went to your hang-out this morning at the bench, and I saw that you and your little group took my advice and decided not to congregate there. Good choice." She patted Lily soundly on the upper arm. "I figured you were the leader, so I guess you get most of the credit."

For what? Lily wanted to say. *For following some rule you made up—that probably isn't even written down?*

She stopped herself in mid-thought.

Wow! What could be more perfect?

"You can go on to class now," Officer Horn said. "I just wanted to tell you that. Value it—I don't hand out that many compliments."

"Could I ask you something?" Lily said.

"Sure." The officer hooked her thumbs in her belt and looked at Lily with eyes that said, *As long as you're seeing things my way now, I'll tell you anything you want to know.*

"Do you have the same list of rules we do? I mean, there aren't any extra ones besides the ones in our student handbooks, are there?"

"Nope. We're not keeping any secrets from you. As long as you follow those rules, you'll be fine."

Lily couldn't hold back a smile. "Thank you," she said. "That's all I needed to know."

Officer Horn wore a smug expression as Lily turned to leave, but it didn't get the prickles going on the back of Lily's neck. She was too busy planning—because she knew exactly what cause to fight for next.

Chapter 6

Zooey's mom had definitely gone all out to turn their basement into a perfect meeting place for the Girlz. For a long time they'd held their meetings in the old playhouse in Reni's backyard, but suddenly, one day they'd all felt cramped in there, with long legs and lanky arms and brand new hips taking up all the room. Zooey's basement definitely had enough space, and after meeting there once, they all decided they liked it. Since then, it had been completely transformed.

Their section was now painted a clear light purple with big yellow, pink, orange, and blue flowers. There was a beanbag chair in each of those colors, a purple long-hair rug to match the walls, and a low table shaped like a big flower—for planning and eating snacks, Zooey told them. Under the table was a basket of markers and a roll of white paper. Over it hung a light with a flower-shaped shade. A bigger basket in the corner, right next to the CD player, held throw pillows. Zooey already had Jars of Clay playing.

"This is amazing!" Reni said. "She did all this for us?"

"She says we should get a lot of encouragement for being such good girls—or something like that." Zooey's eyes were going back and forth, as if she were trying to decide whether to be proud or embarrassed. "I don't know—maybe it's cheesy—"

"No—it's not cheesy at all!" Lily said. "It looks like—us!"

Kresha had already flopped into the bright yellow beanbag and was gurgling like a baby in a bathtub. "Is beautiful, Zo-wee!" she said. "Just like you!"

"Anybody hungry?" Mrs. Hoffman said from the bottom of the steps. She was carrying a tray that was practically groaning with fruit and crackers and cheese in the shape of—what else—flowers.

"There isn't anything gooey and naughty on here," Zooey's mom said as she set the whole feast on the flower table. "Zooey just doesn't do treats anymore."

"But this *is* a treat," Suzy said.

"We feel like princesses, right guys?" Lily said.

They all grinned up at Mrs. Hoffman, and to their dismay, she started to cry.

"That's just what I wanted you to feel like," she said. She squeezed Lily's shoulder as she sniffed. "I can't tell you what it means to me for Zooey to have all of you as her friends."

Nobody knew what to say, least of all, it seemed, Zooey. Her hazel eyes kept getting bigger and bigger until her mom finally thanked them six more times and hurried back upstairs.

"Why was she crying?" Reni whispered.

"She cries all the time," Zooey said.

"I think that was happy crying," Suzy said.

"Well, she's really gonna be happy when she finds out what we're doing next," Lily said. "All our parents are gonna be proud of us. *We're* gonna be proud of us."

"So what is it, already?" Reni said.

Lily smiled at all of them. "I found us a cause."

Nobody except Kresha looked excited. Suzy actually looked like she'd lost her appetite.

"Is it gonna get us in trouble?" Zooey said.

"Did I get in trouble this morning for standing up to Ms. Bavetta?"

"No," Reni said, "but people walk all over Ms. Bavetta all the time. You could probably drop a bomb in her room, and all she would say is 'Claaaass!'"

"Okay—so that's not a good example," Lily said. "But this is a better cause—I promise you."

"Tell Lily," Kresha said. Her eyes were sparkling—at least, the part of them Lily could see under her bangs.

"You know how Deputy Dog told us we couldn't meet together before school?"

"Yeah."

Lily smiled smugly and pulled a book out of her backpack. "You remember this student handbook they gave us at orientation?"

Heads nodded.

"There's no rule in here that says we can't hang out in designated student areas. She made that up. As long as we're not disturbing anyone, we can meet on any of the benches, in the courtyard, or anyplace that's supervised."

"That spot's definitely supervised," Reni said, dimples deepening. "We found that out."

"Exactly! I asked her if she had extra rules that weren't in the handbook, and she said no. As long as we're following these rules," Lily said, giving the book a thump, "we should be okay."

"So are you going to tell her that?" Suzy said. Her delicate eyebrows wrinkled with concern.

"No," Lily said. "*We* are going to *show* her that."

"I don't get it," Zooey said.

"I think I do." Reni put down the banana she was peeling. "You want us to do that past-tense-resuscitation thing, or whatever it's called."

"Passive resistance. We show up at the bench tomorrow morning just like we always did, and we don't bring food—although we might get to that later. We just sit there and talk all quiet and don't disturb anybody."

"But what happens if Officer What's-Her-Name sees us?" Suzy asked, her eyebrows almost meeting in the middle.

"I hope she does," Lily said. "*When* she sees us, she's gonna tell us to move on, and we're just going to tell her that we have a right to stay there and that's what we're going to do. It's simple and peaceful."

"It's not gonna be peaceful at my house when I get hauled down to the office!" Reni said.

"Our parents will stand behind us," Lily said, "because we won't be breaking any rules. Besides, Martin Luther King went to jail for what he believed.

"Jail!" Suzy said.

"If he hadn't, Reni wouldn't even be sitting here with us. We wouldn't be allowed to be friends with her."

"I know of things like that," Kresha said soberly. "They do in my country all the time." Her smile returned. "But *this* is my country now."

"And you wanna live here because we're free to stand up for our rights," Lily said. "We're gonna be advocates for all the other kids who have given up the right to hang out legally where they want to—just because Deputy Dog thinks she's a real cop."

"You don't really think Deputy Dog's gonna give up as easy as Ms. Bavetta, do you?" Reni said.

Lily sighed patiently. "No, and I hope she doesn't, because this is going to give us a chance to really demonstrate passive resistance. When she drags us all down to the office, maybe even bodily—"

"Bodily?" Suzy said. Her face turned milk-white.

"—we won't resist or anything. We'll just go quietly."

"I won't," Zooey said. "I'll be bawling my eyes out!"

"Yeah—that kind of runs in your family," Reni said.

"No, you won't," Lily said to Zooey, "because you'll be happy to be standing up for your rights and the rights of every other kid in the whole entire school."

Zooey pondered that for a second. Then she shook her head and said, "No, I'll be crying."

"Then what?" Reni said. "We go down to the office, and they give us all detention?"

"Detention?" Suzy squeaked.

"Or something worse," Lily said.

"Worse?" Suzy said, now even paler.

"The worse the better," Lily said. "The more they do to us, the bigger the statement we'll be making. That means, of course, that we might have to take drastic measures."

"Drastic?" Suzy's voice was by this time barely audible.

"What is drastic, Lily?" Kresha asked.

"Something big, but never violent. Like, go without food, shave our heads—"

"No way!"

"Come on, Lily!"

"You are so kidding, right?"

Lily waved them all down. "Okay—so we don't all have to go that far—and besides, I don't think we'll have to. As soon as we show them that we haven't broken any rules, it's Deputy Dog who's gonna be in trouble."

"Now that I like," Reni said.

"But that's not why we're doing it," Lily said quickly. "We're not out for revenge."

"Well, that's good at least," Zooey said. With her eyes swimming with tears, she looked a lot like her mother at the moment.

"It's all going to be good," Lily said. "We'll get our place back. Other kids will get theirs. And we'll become known as *advocates*. We might even change our group name."

"I like Girlz Only," Zooey said.

"Me too," Suzy agreed.

They both looked as if they were teetering on the edge of a cliff. Lily reached over and put a hand on each of their knees. "Okay, okay, so we don't change the name. But we don't change our meeting place either."

"But now we have this place, " Suzy said, looking around the flowery basement corner. "This is a lot better."

"But you said yourself you needed to be with all of us before the day started or you couldn't handle it."

"I just wish there was a different way. A way we could do it without getting in trouble."

"This *is* the way not to get in trouble!" The back of Lily's neck was prickling.

Reni looked up from Lily's handbook, which was open in her lap. "Lily's right," she said. "There's no rule against it in here. That does kinda make me mad."

"Me too!" Kresha said.

"Then why don't we vote?" Lily said.

Zooey gave a huge sigh. "Never mind. We already know it's three against two." She looked at Lily through liquid eyes. "As long as you promise this is gonna work out."

"I do," Lily said, raising her hand. "I love you guys. I would never hurt you—ever!"

Zooey looked at Suzy. "Are you in?" she asked.

Suzy's face was pained. "I'm such a chicken."

Kresha looked baffled. "You are fried chicken, Su-zee? Colonel Sanders?"

"No—that means I'm a coward. I'm not brave—"

"Yes, you are," Lily said. "Martin Luther King says cowards run away. Brave people step up to the plate even when they're scared."

"We're all in this together," Reni said.

"And you forgot one thing," Lily reminded them.

"Something else?" Suzy said, voice squeaking even higher.

"We have God on our side. See—I listen to God."

"Wow," Zooey said.

Suzy held out her hands to either side. "Then we better pray."

They got into a circle on their knees and held hands and prayed—for God to give them strength and courage. For him to make Deputy Dog understand—

"—and help Zooey not to pee her pants," Zooey put in.

"Somebody oughta say amen," Lily said.

"Amen!" they all said together.

There was a sniffle from the direction of the stairs.

"All I heard was the 'amen,'" Zooey's mom said. "But I know God heard everything you were saying. You are precious angels from heaven."

Then she left, probably, Lily thought, to get more tissue.

The Girlz dug into the snacks then, and even Suzy seemed to relax a little until Lily said, "We have to talk about what we're going to wear tomorrow."

"What do you mean, wear?" Zooey said.

"We have to wear special clothes?" Suzy said.

Reni grinned at her. "You got anything black-and-white striped? We could all go as prisoners."

"Knock it off, Reni," Zooey said. "You're scaring Suzy again."

"No, now listen," Lily said. "We all look like we wear what our mommies tell us to wear. If we're going up against authority, we have to look like we are our own people."

"Huh?" Zooey said.

"We have to dress like we aren't willing to conform—you know, just do what everybody else does—like do what some monitor tells us even if it's not a rule."

"We're gonna look like a buncha weirdos!" Zooey said.

"No, I think I get it," Reni said. "We wear something we always wanted to wear but we didn't have the nerve."

"Right!" Lily said.

"What if I don't have anything like that?" Suzy said.

"Look in your sister's closet," Reni said. "I already know what I'm wearing."

"What?" Lily said.

"It's a surprise."

"So—it should be something we think somebody might make fun of, only we really want to wear it, right?" Zooey said.

Kresha was bobbing her head up and down. "You say you not smart, Zo-wee—but you are!"

"I'm still not sure," Suzy said.

"Okay—think about this—we'll all stick together, no matter what."

Reni got on one side of her and Kresha on the other. Zooey joined in, giggling and keeping everybody supplied with grapes. Lily watched them and glowed.

I knew they'd come through, she thought happily. *Tomorrow is going to be amazing.*

Chapter 7

Finding something to wear wasn't as easy as Lily thought it would be. Dressing like Gandhi was out. No way she was showing up in Huggies.

Martin Luther King, from what she could tell in the pictures, just wore regular clothes. That didn't look like much fun to Lily.

She was scraping hangers back and forth on the pole in her closet when Mom poked her head into Lily's room.

"I'm putting out an all-points bulletin for dirty dishes," she said. "I'm about to run the dishwasher."

"I don't have any in here," Lily said.

"Art had half a set of silverware in his room. That boy has a hollow leg. What are you doing, Lil?" She moved closer to the closet. "Taking a wardrobe inventory? Do you need new stuff? You're definitely growing like the proverbial weed."

"I'm not a weed, Mom," Lily said. "I'm just looking for something to wear tomorrow."

Mom looked at her watch. "Better hurry. You only have thirteen hours to decide."

Lily stopped her neck in mid-prickle and pulled her head out of the closet.

"Were you ever an advocate, Mom?" she said.

"A what?" Mom's mouth twitched. "I guess not—I'm not even sure what that is."

"Did you ever protest anything, like when you were in college?" Lily said tightly. Why did everything have to be a joke with Mom?

"Oh. No, I missed the sixties and seventies. By the eighties, all anybody cared about was big hair and big bucks." Mom tapped her lips with her fingers. "Now, I was in an anti-abortion march one time."

"What did you wear?"

"What did I *wear*? Honey, I have to look down at myself to remember what I'm wearing right *now*!" She gave a soft grunt. "You poor kid—you got a mother that doesn't know beans about being feminine. Okay—let me think." She paused, and then snapped her fingers. "We all wore T-shirts that said, 'It's a Life, Not a Choice.'"

"Cool," Lily said.

Mom said, "Ding! Correct answer, Mom! First time in two weeks!"

"Mom—"

"It's okay, Lil—I know you're just feeling your Cheerios. As long as you don't get cheeky on me, you're okay."

"Cheeky?" she said.

"Smart-mouthed. I practically had to duct tape Art's mouth closed when he was your age."

"Tape it now, would you?" Lily said.

Mom gave another mouth twitch and left in search of more dirty dishes. Before she reached Joe's room, Lily was already digging in her drawer for a plain T-shirt.

"I wish I had time to make one for all the Girlz," she said to Otto, who was watching her from the bed. "Maybe next time."

Then she forced herself not to sit and imagine them all in Zooey's basement, designing their protest wear, and concentrated on her shirt. She had it almost done by suppertime when Art tapped on her door.

"Time to eat," he said. "What's that smell?"

"Paint," she said.

He craned his neck to look over her bent back. "'We Shall Overcome?'" he read. "What are you gonna overcome, flat-chestedness?"

"No! You are evil!" She held up the T-shirt so he could get a better look. Wet purple, pink, yellow, blue, and orange letters shone in the overhead light. "It's a song blacks sang back in the sixties when they were fighting for their rights."

"Yeah, but Lily, I got a news flash for you: you aren't black."

"Du-uh. You don't have to be black to fight for your rights."

"You doing some kind of project for school?"

"Something like that," Lily said. She paused. *Maybe I oughta tell Art*, she thought. *He knows a lot of stuff—*

"Did you have to memorize that 'I Have a Dream' speech?" Art was saying. "Dude, we did—a big old chunk of it. I had Mrs. Boline. You're lucky she left to go have a kid or something."

Never mind, Lily thought. *He's not ready for this.*

But Lily was, and the next morning she put her new T-shirt on with her carpenter jeans and surveyed herself in the mirror.

I do look different, she thought. *No more Anne of Green Gables. Call me—Rosa Parks!*

"It finally feels like fall out there," Mom called from the stairs. "Put on a sweater or something, Lil. Let's go."

Lily grabbed her jacket and put it on as she ran for the car. Nobody had to tell her twice—she'd never *been* so anxious to get to school.

None of the Girlz was there when she reached the bench, or so she thought. She barely had time to put down her backpack when all four of them appeared as if out of nowhere.

"Where were you?" Lily said.

"Around," Reni said.

"We were scared to stand here together until you got here," Zooey said.

"Oh," Lily said. "So let's see what everybody's wearing."

Coats and sweaters came off, and Lily gazed at the display in front of her.

Reni had on a long tunic and baggy pants in brilliant colors with beads to match around her throat.

"This is traditional African attire," she said, tilting her chin proudly.

"It looks like pajamas," Zooey said.

"No it doesn't!" Lily said—although it actually did.

She went on to Kresha. She was wearing a dress. It looked like it might have come from Kmart, but she looked pretty in it.

"Nobody vear a dress here," Kresha said. "I like to vear dress. DressES."

"It's cute," Suzy said. "You guys all came up with neat stuff. I feel dumb now."

"Let's see," Zooey said.

Suzy took off her long jacket as if she'd been asked to disrobe completely and stood stiffly in front of them, head hanging down.

"It's great!" Reni said.

"Wow," Zooey said.

Kresha was nodding enthusiastically.

Lily had to agree—with all of the above.

Plain little please-don't-notice-me Suzy had on slightly baggy jeans, red clunky-heeled shoes, and a cherry red turtleneck. It made her look like she was actually getting a figure.

"My sister picked it out," Suzy said. "I always wanted to be outgoing like she is."

"You *are* outgoing," Zooey said.

"No, she's not!" said the other three.

"But it doesn't matter," Lily said quickly. "We like you just the way you are."

"Do you think this is the way we *really* are?" Reni said, panning the group with her eyes. "Now that we're wearing what we really *want* to?"

"We haven't seen everybody's yet," Suzy said.

"Here's mine," Lily said. She pulled open her jacket to reveal her T-shirt.

They all blinked at it.

"Do you like it?" Lily said. "Because I was thinking we could all have one like it for next time."

"Next time?" Suzy said.

Reni nudged Lily. "Maybe we oughta just get through this time, huh?"

"Wanna see mine?" Zooey said. She shed her jacket and turned around to face them. She was wearing a sweatshirt that had the letters WWJD on it.

"It stands for 'What Would Jesus Do,'" she said.

"Du-uh," Reni said.

"Well, you said we should wear something we always wanted to but we didn't because we thought people would make fun of us for it."

"It's perfect," Suzy said.

"Yeah," Lily said.

Reni was frowning. "You're *sure* Jesus would want us doing this?"

"I told you—I listen to God," Lily said.

"Wow," Zooey said. "I listen too, only I never hear anything. How do you do that?"

"I'll tell you later," Lily said. "Let's sit down. We have to be looking all peaceful when Deputy Dog comes by."

"Could we start calling her Officer Horn?" Suzy said as they formed a sit-down circle on the ground. "I'm afraid I'm gonna mess up and call her Deputy Dog to her face sometime."

"Don't worry," Lily said. "After today, I don't think we're ever gonna have to deal with her again."

"Yeah," Reni said. "She's gonna totally leave us alone."

"Sh!" Zooey said. "Here she comes!"

"Already?" Suzy squeaked.

Kresha grabbed onto her hand. Zooey took the other one. Pretty soon, they were all clinging to each other's fingers. Suzy and Zooey squeezed their eyes shut.

"What is this?" said the familiar voice. "A séance?"

Lily fixed a polite smile on her face and looked up at Officer Horn. "No," she said. "We're just sitting here—peacefully."

"Not disturbing anybody," Reni added.

"I don't know about that," Office Horn said. She put one foot up on the bench and leaned on her thigh. "I'm a little disturbed by what I'm seeing."

Suzy squeaked. Nobody else said a word.

"I distinctly remember telling all five of you day before yesterday that you were not to congregate here anymore. And I *know* I told you, Robbins, that I was pleased to see you took my advice." She made a clicking sound with her mouth. "Now it looks like you've changed your minds."

Lily felt a chill go up her spine where the prickles usually were. This was sort of like getting on a ride in Atlantic City. She tried not to sound too excited as she said, "We have changed our minds. We read the student handbook."

"Well, excuse me for not breaking out into applause," Office Horn said. "We don't hand them out just to add to your locker decor."

"I know," Lily said. "We studied it, and Officer Horn, did you know that it says students may meet informally in designated areas?" She nodded at Reni.

"And did you know that this is a desig—this is one of those areas?" Reni said.

Officer Horn slowly lowered her leg from the bench.

Here it comes, Lily thought. *She's either gonna back down or drag us all to the office. This is it—*

"And did you know that I have the right to interpret those rules as I see fit?" Officer Horn said. "Does anybody have said handbook on her person at this time?"

"We all do!" Zooey said. She grabbed for hers and tried to wave it, but it slipped out of her hand and onto Officer Horn's toe. The officer picked up the handbook and, glowering at the Girlz over the top of it, licked her thumb and flipped through the pages.

What is she talking about? Reni's eyes said to Lily.

I don't know, Lily's said back. *But it'll be fine. She's bluffing.*

"Ah, here we are." Officer Horn squatted down and said, "I quote: 'Any school official or legal officer of the school board'—that would be me—'may at any time enforce conduct not specifically stated in these rules. Such conduct would be any behavior that is disturbing or distracting to the student body as a whole.'" She looked up. "End quote."

"But what does that *mean*?" Zooey said. And she started to cry.

"It means if I *say* you're disturbing or distracting other students by being here, then you *are*." She looked over her shoulder. "Look at the crowd you're drawing."

"Oh," Suzy said. She'd gone beyond milk-white. There was a frost of fear on her face.

Lily looked up at the quickly growing group of people who were stopping on the way to their classes and lockers to stare.

Good, she thought. *We're getting the attention we wanted. This is good.*

At least it was until she saw Shad Shifferdecker go by. Ashley Adamson was with him, and she dragged him to a stop at the edge of the crowd. The laughing and pointing started immediately.

That's okay, Lily told herself. *People like that don't bother me anymore. They should dream of being as brave as we are.*

"Not only that," Officer Horn was saying, "but now you've attracted *my* attention too, and I've noticed that some of you are not attired according to the dress code."

"She's wearing her pajamas!" Ashley Adamson called out, pointing at Reni.

"I don't need any help from the peanut gallery, thank you," Officer Horn said dryly. "You people move on before I write everybody up."

They scattered like ants, except for Shad, who sauntered off behind Ashley as if "moving on" had been his own idea.

"They do look like pajamas," Officer Horn said to Reni.

"It's African," Reni said. Lily's stomach stirred. Reni's voice was sounding a little shaky.

"Well, unless you're celebrating Kwanza in one of your classes, I'm going to send you to the office for a change of clothes."

Lily didn't have a chance to see how Reni reacted before Officer Horn turned on Kresha. "You're within the code, but learn how to sit like a lady, would you? This isn't a Third World country."

Now the prickles started, and Lily didn't put a hand up to stop them. She could only stare at Officer Horn.

"Now you, Missy," she said to Suzy, "are pushing the envelope, though technically you're okay. But if the boys start making wolf calls, don't come crying to me about harassment."

Lily knew poor Suzy didn't have any idea what she was talking about. She was staring straight ahead of her, shaking like a loose pine needle. Lily's entire backbone was one huge set of syringes.

"You're allowed to profess your faith," Officer Horn was saying to Zooey, "but you're asking for trouble if you go around advertising like that."

Finally, she turned to Lily, who was by now stiff from sneakers to hair scrunchie.

"And what have we here? 'We Shall Overcome.' What is it you're trying to overcome, Robbins? A decent education? Somebody who wants to teach you to respect authority?" She didn't give Lily a chance to answer, but turned to the whole group. "You ladies can relax," she said. "I'm not going to write you up or send you to the office for dress code violations or anything else today. But you just got a taste of what it's going to be like if you continue to defy me. All this attitude is going to get you is *me* all over you for every little thing you do. Is that understood?"

Kresha, Reni, Zooey, and Suzy all nodded their heads.

"All right," Officer Horn said. "Now get out of here, all of you. And I repeat, don't hang out together before school. You see what kind of trouble it gets you into."

Zooey immediately began to scramble up, but Lily put her hand on her knee.

"You wanted to say something else, Robbins?" Officer Horn said.

"Yes," Lily said. "I wanted to say—" She took a deep breath. The prickles stabbed at her. "I want to say no. We're not going anywhere."

Chapter 8

Lily had never seen horror before, but she knew she was seeing it now—on the faces of the Girlz as they stared at her.

This was our plan, she said back to them with her eyes.

Nobody else seemed to remember that. Zooey was sobbing louder than ever, and Suzy looked completely frozen.

"Okay, you guys," Reni said. "Come on."

She stood up. It was Lily's turn to stare.

"There's somebody with some sense," Officer Horn said. "Come on, ladies, I don't like to be a hardnose. I'm just trying to keep you from getting yourselves into trouble."

"What trouble?" Lily said. She was still trying to keep her voice polite, but it was getting harder. "All we're doing is sitting here."

"It's okay, Lily," Zooey said. "Let's just go."

She got up with Suzy still clinging to her. Reni herded them toward the lockers with her head. Kresha was the only one left sitting.

"You going, Lily?" Kresha said.

"No," Lily said coldly. "You go ahead if you want to, but I'm staying here."

"You know what, girls, let her stay," Officer Horn said. "With all of you gone, she can sit here until the bell rings—all by herself." She hooked her thumbs onto her belt. "Like I said, there are things you'll do in a group that you'd never think of doing by yourself. Go on—shoo. You have ten minutes before first period. You must have *something* to do."

The Girlz, including Kresha, moved slowly toward the lockers, all of them looking back over their shoulders. Lily tried not to look at any of them. Her heart was pounding, but she kept her eyes steady on Officer Horn's belt buckle and tried to stay calm.

I don't care if she drags me to the office by the hair, Lily thought. *I'm going to stay here until the bell rings. I have my rights. Yeah—I do.*

But the voice in her head was shaking, and she had to latch her hands around her knees to keep *them* from quivering. It had been so much easier with the Girlz around her.

Officer Horn squatted until her face was level with Lily's.

"Your friends are smart, Robbins," she said. "They all left. You can have this spot now all by your lonesome. Why don't you sit right here and think about how far you really want to carry this little game?"

"It's not a game!"

"Watch your tone."

Lily clenched her teeth together. "We never did anything wrong. I'm just standing up for my rights."

"You go ahead and do your little thing," Officer Horn said. Her voice was rough. "But remember what I said. You pull attitude with me—I'm going to pull hardnose with you. From here on, I'll be watching you. Any little infraction, and you're going down."

She stood up. Lily shifted her eyes to her knees.

"I don't want to do this," Officer Horn said, her voice a fraction less like sandpaper. "But if it's the only way to make you see that your energy's being channeled in the wrong direction, then that's the way it'll be. One more chance to make a better choice?"

She waited. Lily imagined herself getting up, muttering an apology, slinking off to the lockers where the Girlz would be waiting for her.

"This *is* my choice," Lily said. "But thanks for asking."

"Have it your way, then. But you better watch your back."

Lily waited until she was gone to get up. Her legs felt like rubber bands. She started to sink down onto the bench in despair, but the thought struck her that Deputy Dog might be peeking out from behind the stairs, just to see if she'd gotten to her.

And she hasn't, Lily told herself. *This is just the way it is when you're an advocate. Nobody said it would be easy.*

Actually, she remembered, she herself had told the Girlz it *would* be easy. Slinging her backpack on, she headed for the lockers, head up, eyes straight ahead, just in case D. D. *was* spying on her.

The Girlz were all at their lockers in a line, fidgeting with the locks as if they all wanted an alibi for standing there. When Reni saw Lily, she dropped her backpack and put her hands on her hips.

"What were you thinkin'?" she said.

"I was thinking I was doing what we all said we were gonna do!" Lily said.

"I told you I couldn't do it, Lily," Suzy said. "I told you I was chicken."

"Me too," Zooey said. Lily saw that she was still hanging on to Suzy's hand. "She just looked so *mean*! I didn't think she'd look so mean."

"Look," Reni said, letting her hands slide from their indignant position, "it was just harder when we were actually doing it. And all I could think of was All-State Orchestra."

"Orchestra?" Lily said, her neck prickling. "What's that got to do with it?"

"There's this committee that decides who gets to go, and Mr. Lamb recommends people from our school. He's not gonna pick me to send to the committee if I've been in trouble. He says they only want to take people who are, like, squeaky-clean."

"You didn't seem too worried about that yesterday," Lily said. She could feel her eyes narrowing.

"That was before this all went down the way it did! When we were just talking about it, I thought she was either gonna give up or take us to the office, and then we were gonna explain it all to the principal or something and it was gonna be all over." Reni pulled off her tunic, revealing a T-shirt underneath. "But when she said she was gonna follow us around and try to nab us for stuff, I got really scared. Nobody can be perfect all the time, Lily! She was bound to catch me doing some stupid little thing, and then I wouldn't get to go to State."

"And I would be take—taken—out of the real classes," Kresha said.

"And my mom would start bawlin'," Zooey said—through her sobs.

Suzy opened her mouth, but Lily cut her off.

"So you're just going to let her violate our rights," she said. She knew her face was going blotchy.

"Lily, come on!" Reni said. "She's practically the police!"

"Let's just meet at my house instead," Zooey said.

"Yeah," Suzy said. "I'll be all right. We don't have to meet here just because of me."

"It's *not* just because of you!" Lily said. "It's the principle of the thing!"

"The principal?" Kresha said. "You going to go to the principal?"

"No!"

"Sh!" Zooey said. "You're gonna have that evil lady over here!"

"And what would you all do?" Lily said. "Run away and leave me standing alone—again?"

She was breathing hard, and her hands were shaking. Suzy was backing up against the locker, and both Zooey and Kresha looked as if they'd just been slapped. Only Reni stepped up to her.

"You could have walked away with us, Lily," she said. "Nobody made you stay there."

"And nobody's making me stay *here*, either!" Lily said. Hitching her backpack angrily on her shoulder, she stomped away.

But where she was going, she had no idea. Her eyes were too blurry to see.

That was the way she went through the rest of the morning—in a blur. If she looked around, she saw one of the Girlz around a corner or across a classroom, and that hurt too much. It was just easier to keep everything a blur.

But when lunchtime came, Lily saw things all too clearly.

The Girlz were all gathered at their usual table. Lily could see them from the doorway where she stood with her brown bag, trying to decide what to do.

I told them I didn't want to be with them if they were gonna be cowards, she thought miserably. *But maybe they've changed their minds by now. I should go find out.*

She took a step inside the cafeteria, and then hesitated again. *But they were the ones who ran out on* me! *Shouldn't they come to me— and apologize?*

No, she told herself firmly as she made her way around a knot of eighth graders and moved closer to the table. That was lame. These were the Girlz. It didn't matter who apologized first—as long as they were together.

But what about the principle of the thing?

Lily stopped yet again and pretended to be digging into her pocket for change.

What *was* the principle of the thing? That they should be allowed to hang around together if they wanted to.

An ache of loneliness formed in Lily's chest. *But we're not together! I'm here and they're there—and that was* my *choice!*

Lily abandoned the search for imaginary quarters and, straightening her shoulders, headed for the table, eyes on her Girlz. They did look bummed out, all of them picking at their sandwiches and chewing listlessly on their chips. Zooey's eyes were so red and puffy you could barely see them.

Lily took the last few steps almost at a run. But she wasn't quick enough. Just as she was about to maneuver around the last clump of people, another figure approached the table. It was Deputy Dog.

Lily stopped and sat down abruptly at the end of the closest table. Officer Horn was standing over the Girlz, thumbs hooked, as always, onto her belt. She wasn't a tall woman—in fact, she reminded Lily of a fire hydrant—but she loomed large as she looked down at them. And they all seemed to shrink, right before Lily's eyes.

With the noise of kids getting all their talking in before they had to hush up for afternoon classes, Lily couldn't hear what Officer Horn was saying, but from the looks on the Girlz' faces as they stared down at the table, she wasn't commending them for their good cafeteria behavior. Only Kresha was looking up at her, and her eyes were glittering in a way Lily had never seen before. She actually looked angry.

Deputy Dog didn't stay long. She patted Suzy on the shoulder as she moved on, and as soon as she was gone, Kresha reached over and brushed at Suzy with her hand as if to remove cooties.

Lily didn't think twice now. Backbone prickling double-time, she lurched out of the seat and was at the Girlz table in three steps.

"What did she say to you?" Lily said—instead of hi.

"Don't talk so loud, Lily!" Zooey said. "You'll have her back over here."

Kresha snarled something in Croatian and glared over her shoulder.

"Scoot over, Reni," Lily said. She wanted to sit down before Deputy Dog saw her and nabbed her for illegal standing in an eating establishment or something.

But Reni didn't move. "No," she said to her tray.

"Fine!" Lily said. "Suzy, would you move over so I can sit down? Hurry before she looks over here."

Suzy looked at Reni, and Reni shook her head.

"What's going on?" Lily said. Zooey put her finger to her lips, but Lily ignored her. "Why can't I sit down?"

"Because that voman is evil!" Kresha said.

"You tell her, Reni," Zooey said. Her eyes were filling up again.

Reni still didn't look at Lily. "She said she couldn't tell us who to hang around with—but she was glad to see we weren't having lunch with you, and she said the more we stayed away from you, the better, because you were gonna get us in trouble."

"That's against the law or something!" Lily said. Her backbone felt like one large cactus. "She can't do that!"

"She was just giving us advice," Reni said. "She said she couldn't bust us for being with you, but that until you straightened up, she was gonna be watching you, and that meant she would be watching us too, as long as you were with us."

"You're not gonna listen to her, are you?" Lily said.

She knew she was nearly screaming, but she didn't care. Zooey obviously did, because she reached up and put her hand on Lily's mouth. Lily smacked it away.

"I don't *want* to listen to her," Reni said. She looked up at Lily for the first time. "But you know how much I want to be picked for All-State. I can't get in any trouble, Lily."

"You won't!" Lily said. "It's not like we're these losers or something! We follow every stinkin' rule in this stupid school!"

"She'll think of something," Reni said. "She's out to get you, Lily. And if we hang out together at school, she'll be out to get us too."

Lily stared at her. "You mean, you're going to do what she says? You're not going to be with me at school—ever?"

"Just 'til All-State—"

"We can talk to you, like in classes and stuff," Suzy said.

"And we'll meet every day in my basement," Zooey said. "My mom'll let us."

"Well—I can't meet *every* day," Reni said, "'cause of orchestra."

"And I have soccer and gymnastics—" Suzy said.

"Wait!" Lily held her hands up like a crossing guard. The Girlz froze. "If you guys don't want to be seen with me in school, then you don't want to be seen with me anywhere."

"Yes, we do," Suzy said.

"Well—I don't!" Lily could feel her eyes blazing down at them. She knew her face was crimson and her voice was loud. She also had a feeling half the cafeteria was looking up from their chip bags to stare at her. But all she saw were the four pained faces in front of her.

She lowered her voice. "If you don't want to be with me here, then I don't want to be with you, ever. We're either in this together or we're not. That's the way it's always been."

Suzy and Zooey looked at Reni. "It can't be that way right now," Reni said.

"Fine," Lily said. For once there were no more words. She could only snatch up her brown bag and march away.

"I say that vould happen," she heard Kresha say.

"Said," Suzy corrected her.

"I *said*! And I vas right!"

But Kresha didn't run after Lily. Lily was alone as she left the cafeteria—more alone than she'd ever been in her life.

Chapter 9

The rest of the day went on without Lily. She felt as if she were standing outside of everything, looking on but not being a part of it. It made her whole body ache.

The minute she got home, she went straight to her room and got out her journal. She didn't even talk to Otto—even when he dumped the hairless tennis ball, his latest soup bone, and one of Joe's chewed-up soccer socks into her lap. All she wanted to do was talk to God.

"They've abandoned me!" she wrote in her journal. "I'm doing what's right—I listen to you everyday and do what you tell me—and now I've lost all my friends. Who am I gonna hang out with now? What am I gonna do before school? Who will I eat lunch with? Who's gonna be in groups with me in classes? I'm never gonna find friends like them again—"

"Lil?"

Lily looked up at the doorway, but she couldn't see who was there through her tears. It was Art's voice, though, talking through the blur.

"What's wrong with you? You look awful."

"Thanks," Lily said. She couldn't think of a funny comeback. Nothing was ever going to be funny again.

"Dude—what happened? Did you get busted at school for flunking a test or something?"

Lily looked up at him sharply. "No—why did you ask that?"

Art sat on the edge of her desk. "Because that's the only reason I can think of for you to be bawlin' your eyes out. You're such a goody-two-shoes and everything."

"No, I'm not!"

"Okay! Dude—chill." He cocked his red head. "You don't have boy trouble, do ya?"

"No! I hate boys!"

"Oh. Well—I'll be goin' then."

He started to get up, but Lily put out her hand. "No—stay," she said. Suddenly being alone sounded like the worst thing on earth.

Art shrugged and propped a foot on her desk chair. "Okay— twenty questions—animal, vegetable, or mineral?"

"School!"

"Ah—animal. Beast, in fact. Okay—academics, athletics, or extracurricular?"

"None of those."

"None of the above—okay. School policy."

"What's that?"

"Rules and stuff," Art said.

"Yes!"

"Then you did get busted."

"No! Well—" Lily cocked her own head. "Define 'busted.'"

"It's pretty broad, actually. It includes referrals, detention, suspension—but it also covers a teacher marking down your citizenship grade or some hall monitor giving you grief."

"Okay—then I got busted."

"Let me guess—Officer Horn."

Lily stared. By now the tears were gone, and she could clearly see her brother grinning at her from across the room, his blue eyes twinkling.

"How'd you know?" she said.

"She's like an institution over at Middle. She was strikin' fear into the hearts of seventh graders when *I* was going there."

"She's not striking any fear in *my* heart," Lily said.

"Oh—so there's *another* reason why you're sitting here having a nervous breakdown."

"She won't let me hang out with the Girlz at school!" Lily blurted out.

"She can't do that."

"Yes, she can! She told them if they kept hanging with me, they'd all get in trouble sooner or later."

"You being the gang leader and all that."

"But we're not a gang!"

"In her mind, everybody over age nine is a potential Mafia member, okay?" Art folded his arms comfortably and leaned back against the wall. "See, the thing with Deputy Dog is she just tries to make her job easier. She thinks if she can break up trouble before it starts, she won't have to work so hard. Give her 'til Christmas—she softens up after that."

"Christmas!" Lily's eyes blurred again. "I can't wait 'til Christmas to have friends again!"

"Okay, okay, there are other ways."

"Like what?"

"You can go one of two ways, actually. You can either be totally clean, go all out to follow all the rules to the letter—*or* you can go the other direction and push the envelope as far as you can without being written up."

"How do I do that?" Lily said.

"That's a good start." Art nodded at the T-shirt she still had on. "Did you wear that to school today?"

"Yeah. But you made fun of it yesterday."

"It makes a statement. A middle-school statement, but still—you're showin' 'em what you're about."

"Oh."

"Just don't pierce anything or get a tattoo," Art said. "You can really mess yourself up doing that. Other than that—anything you can think of goes—as long as you don't go outside the rules."

"So I'm just trying to get them to pay attention to what I'm trying to say."

"Something like that."

Lily felt better, but there was still one thing—one thing that made her shoulders sag. "But what about the Girlz? They're doing that other thing—you know, doing exactly what they're told. I'm all by myself now."

"Yeah, that's a bummer—but you're making a choice. Hey, life's full of tough choices." He shook his sixteen-year-old head wisely. "You can come to me, though. I mean, not like out in public—but here in the house. I'll help you out. I've been there, remember?"

"Yeah," Lily said. She watched in amazement as he gave her a thumbs-up sign and strolled his tall self out the door. Then she sighed. It was still lonely. She was so used to having a group that rallied around her projects. Not having a single friend to be with was going to be the tough part.

It got even tougher the next day. Saturday morning wasn't so bad because the whole family went out into the yard right after breakfast and finished up the leaf-raking.

"Looks like we get to go to the Eagles game tomorrow!" Joe said as his last bushel went into the wheelbarrow.

"Like they weren't gonna take us anyway," Art said. "They've had the tickets forever."

"I don't know about that," Mom said. "We could always ask somebody else to go."

"No way!" Joe said. "Where are the seats—fifty-yard line?"

"Far up enough so we can see the plays?" Art said. "You get too low and you lose perspective."

"I'm thinking about the hot dogs," Dad said. "I'm not going to worry about cholesterol at all tomorrow."

"Let's have a contest!" Joe said. "See who can eat the most."

"Blech," Mom said, mouth twitching.

Dad looked at Lily. "You don't seem too excited, Liliputian."

"I have a lot on my mind," Lily said.

"This will be a good distraction for you, Lil," Mom said. "A bunch of yelling and screaming is good for your soul."

"Besides," Dad said, "it's Family Day. You used to love those."

"You used to *plan* those," Art said. "I'm glad you're out of that phase. Remember the art museum?"

"Bo-ring!" Joe said.

Lily glared at him, but that was all. She didn't have the energy to fight with him. She had to save it for the cause.

"Can I go now?" Lily said. "I've got stuff to do in my room."

Once she got up there, though, it was hard to concentrate. She kept waiting for the phone to ring, hoping it would be Reni or Suzy—

It never was. About five o'clock, she felt the tears building again. She tried writing in her journal, but there was nothing different to say to God.

I have to keep trying, though, she told herself. *I've forgotten about God before, and I'm not doing it this time.*

That helped until at supper, Mom said, "Everybody wear what you're going to wear to the game to church so we can leave right from there. The traffic's going to be a bear."

Church. Lily set down her forkful of baked beans. Reni would be at church, and so would Suzy. They'd be in the same Sunday school class—only the three of them wouldn't be together. The two of them would whisper to each other, but not to her. They'd giggle, but she wouldn't know what it was about.

But it's not school, she thought. *Nobody at church will be telling them I'm going to get them in trouble with the pastor!*

And then her own words rang in her head, clanging like some too-loud bell: *If you don't want to be with me, then I don't want to be with you—EVER!*

"Having an argument with yourself, Lil?" Mom said.

Lily bristled. "Do I *have* to go to church tomorrow?" she said. "Can't you pick me up on the way to the game?"

"Excuse me?" Mom said.

She and Dad exchanged parent glances across the table.

"If she gets to stay home, so do I!" Joe said.

"Down boy," Dad said. "Nobody's staying home."

"Be there, or be square, Lil," Mom said. But there was no twitching around her mouth.

After supper, Lily couldn't force herself to go back up to her room again. The walls were starting to feel like they were closing in. She put on a sweater and parked herself on the front porch. The trees had pretty much dumped all their leaves by now, and they looked naked and exposed. Mom had put an arrangement of pumpkins and chrysanthemums by the steps, and Lily tried to concentrate on that. It seemed like the only bright spot.

"Hey, Lily," Joe said, hanging out the screen door. "Phone's for you. Here—catch."

He tossed her the portable phone, and she nearly missed it. Her hands had already started to sweat.

Taking a huge breath, she said, "Hello?"

"Lily?"

It was Kresha. Lily gripped the receiver.

79

"Yeah—Kresh?"

"Hi. I am calling you."

"I know." Lily hardly dared to ask, but she said, "What's up?"

"I think they wrong, Lily. They *are* wrong, I mean. The Girlz."

"You do?" Lily said. Her palms were so sweaty now she had to cradle the phone in her neck and wipe her hands on her sweatpants. "Do you mean that?"

"Ya. They not—no, they don't know about stand up for right. My family—ve do."

"You mean, like in Croatia?"

"Ya. Lily?"

"Ya—I mean, yeah?"

"I vant be—I vant to be—your friend."

"You are!"

"I vant to be vit you—*with* you—at school."

"You do?"

Lily knew she was answering every statement with a question, but she had to make sure. In fact, she asked another one.

"But you know, don't you, that if you hang out with me, the other Girlz won't want to be with you?"

"Ya. I know. But we got to do vat's right, Lily."

"Oh, Kresha! I love you!"

"Okay. Dat's vat I vant to say."

"It's gonna be hard, though," Lily said. "I already know after only, like, one day."

"So—you gotta plan?"

"A plan?" Lily said.

"You alvays got plan, Lily."

"Oh—yeah, I do, don't I?" She was giggling for no particular reason, other than that the loneliness was dissolving. She wanted to keep Kresha on the phone all night.

"You vant to come to my house tomorrow?" Kresha said. "So ve can make a plan?"

"Yes!" Lily said. "My brother told me what to do too, so I've got a lot of ideas! This is gonna be so cool—I didn't want to do it alone, Kresha."

"Ya."

So Kresha gave Lily directions to the apartment where she lived with her mom and two brothers. It wasn't in the best part of town, but Lily knew Mom and Dad wouldn't mind. They'd always encouraged her to make friends with minority people if she liked them and they were good people. And Kresha was the best—

"I'll come right after church," Lily said.

They said their good-byes and hung up, and Lily sank back into the porch swing with a sigh—a happy sigh this time.

But happiness was like a bubble lately. It never seemed to stay for more than ten seconds. For there was Mom, pulling her sweater over her chest as she sat down beside Lily.

"You'll come where right after church?" Mom said.

"To Kresha's," Lily said. "You don't know everything that's happened, Mom. All the other girls have dumped me, except Kresha. She invited me over so we can—"

"Tomorrow. After church."

"Yeah."

"What else is happening tomorrow after church?"

"Oh," Lily said. "The football game. But Mom—I don't really want to go to that. You know I'm not into sports. You said you could always give the ticket to somebody else. Maybe Art's girlfriend—"

"It's 'family day,' Lil. You're part of the family."

"But, Mom, this is important!"

"And we're not?"

"Well, yeah, but this is *more* important!"

"Oh, I don't think so." Mom's mouth was perfectly straight. "Right now, I don't think you know what's important—and that's okay—everybody has to go through that at your age. But your Dad and I have to guide you through it, and that means once in a while, we'll make a decision you don't like."

"But I don't get it!"

"I know. That's the problem. You've developed this attitude that, frankly, we're not crazy about. It's as if we are all a big nuisance that you have to put up with."

"But I want to be with my friend!"

"Another time," Mom said. She stood up. "Tomorrow, you're going to be with us."

Chapter 10

Lily had never spent a more miserable day than that Sunday. The Eagles won the game. Art won the hot-dog-eating contest. But Lily felt as if she'd lost out on absolutely everything. By the time they finally pulled in the driveway, after stopping for an endless dinner at the Londonshire, she was more determined than ever to do something her own way.

"Nobody understands what I'm going through, God," she wrote in her journal, "except maybe Art, definitely Kresha—and you."

There was one other possibility, though, which she forgot until the next day in first period when Ms. Bavetta handed her a note.

"Coming to see me second period today?" Mr. Miniver had written.

Yes! Lily thought. *Why didn't I think of him before?*

Ms. Bavetta's perfume suddenly smelled closer. "Are you seeing Mr. Miniver for counseling?" she said.

Lily nodded.

"Good," she said, and moved on.

Actually, it's not exactly counseling, Lily wanted to say to her. *He's my friend. We just talk. He understands me.*

But the note made her feel that maybe things weren't so bad after all. She dug into her backpack for a Girlz-Gram form. Suzy's mom had made photocopies and given each girl a handful. It was the perfect way to write quick notes to each other. They hadn't written many last week—it had been such a different week. But now it was time.

TO: Kresha

Meet after second at lockers. May have ideas.

It was with a light heart that Lily checked in with her study-hall teacher and hurried down to Mr. Miniver's conference-room office. He had two Diet Dr. Peppers waiting and popped hers open. As he handed the can to her, his eyes went to her shirt. It looked a little worse for wear after having been rinsed out over the weekend, but Lily displayed it proudly.

"I made it myself," she said. "It's part of being an advocate."

"Uh-huh," Mr. Miniver said. He sipped at his soda, leaving bubbles popping on his mustache. "What are we going to overcome, Lily-Pad?"

"A whole bunch of stuff," Lily said. And then, setting her soda can back on the table, she told him the whole story.

When she was finished, Mr. Miniver took another drink. Lily couldn't help feeling that he was stalling. There was no twinkle in his eye.

"Are you sure that's your best course of action?" he asked.

"Yes!" Lily said. But she felt herself sagging inside. "Don't you?"

"It's more important what *you* think now," he said. "You're obviously at the place where you're not going to be happy just doing what you're told. I think you'll do it, because that's the way you've been brought up, but I don't think you'll *like* it, unless you can feel inside yourself that it's right and just and all those things."

"What's wrong with that?" Lily said. She was beginning to get a little prickly—but this was Mr. Miniver!

"Nothing. But I think you're making things pretty hard on yourself."

"Excuse me—I don't mean to be rude or anything," Lily said. "But I'm not the one making it hard. It's my parents, and Officer Horn, and my teachers, and even the Girlz. I told you, Kresha's the only one who gets it."

"Kresha comes from a different background. And she definitely doesn't have the Christian training you've had."

"I thought we couldn't talk about being Christians here at school."

Mr. Miniver smiled—but just a little. "We can if we're both Christians and we're not trying to push it on anyone else."

"That's so not fair. I think I'm gonna work on that next as an advocate."

"Let's stick with your current cause, shall we?" Mr. Miniver said. "Now—you say you want to be an advocate."

"I am!"

"Okay—but it seems to me that right now, you need an advocate yourself."

"I have you—don't I?"

Mr. Miniver looked her in the eye. He was more serious than she had ever seen him. "I was thinking of Jesus, Lily."

"Oh," Lily said. She could still feel the prickles on her neck. "But I pray to God every day—all the time! I'm doing what he says to do."

"Really? God told you to go to the farthest extreme you can get away with to make your point? He told you to turn away from your good Christian friends? He said, 'Lily, be aggravated with your parents, because they don't understand you anymore'? He said all that to you?"

"Well—yeah. I mean, he sent me Art. That had to be a God-thing. Art doesn't come in my room every day and give me advice. And he sent me Kresha—she's on my side."

"Whoa," Mr. Miniver said. "I don't think God ever told anybody to choose up sides."

"That's what he told me," Lily said through her teeth. "I listened, and that's what I heard."

"I think what you heard was what you wanted to hear. You have an agenda, Lily, and you listened until somebody else agreed with it, and you called that God."

"Nuh-uh!" Lily said. She could feel hot tears springing to her eyes, and she hated that. In fact, right now, she just about hated everything.

Mr. Miniver didn't seem to notice the tears or the hate. "There's always the possibility that I'm wrong," he said. "The only way you're going to know is to listen to God—and the only way you're going to be able to do that is to let Jesus be your advocate."

Lily didn't know what else to do but pick up the Dr. Pepper can and drain it. She wanted to scream at him that he was wrong. She wanted to hurl the can across the room. But she couldn't do anything she really wanted to do.

Except what she'd already planned.

She set the can down slowly and dabbed at her mouth with her fingers.

"Well, thanks for the advice, Mr. Miniver," she said. "I'll think about it."

"Let me give you some *ways* to think about it," he said. "I don't know about you, but I have a little trouble sometimes knowing how to see what Jesus is trying to tell me. Why don't you start with 1 John 2—and then, of course, read about any time Jesus stuck up for somebody—how about John, I think it's chapter 8, where he tells the people to let one who hasn't ever sinned cast the first stone."

"Okay, thanks," Lily said. "I'll read it before I come in next time. Day after tomorrow?"

He looked at her for a moment before he nodded. His mustache was a little droopy as he said, "You're a fine young woman, Lily-Pad. We all just want you to stay that way."

"Okay," Lily said.

Mr. Miniver looked like he was going to add something else, but he pressed his lips together and nodded. The twinkle was gone from his eyes.

When second period finally ended, Lily waited at the lockers for Kresha. She'd thought Mr. Miniver was going to give her some ideas, but that hadn't worked out.

Still, she thought, *I know for sure now that Kresha and I are doing the right thing. Adults just don't get it, and we have to show them.*

When Kresha rushed up to her, Lily steered her around the bank of lockers, just in case the other Girlz showed up.

"Ve are hiding?" Kresha said.

"No," Lily said. "We just don't want to stir things up right now. We have plans to make. I'm sorry I couldn't come over yesterday—you got my message, right?"

Kresha nodded. "It gives you a pain to see them, ya?"

"Who—Reni and them? A pain?" Lily started to shake her head, but Kresha's eyes seemed to see right through her, even from behind her straggly bangs. "Yeah, it does," Lily said. "We've been friends a long time. But we're gonna fix that. They're gonna see that we're right and they're gonna respect us so much they'll want to do what we're doing."

"Vat are ve doing?" Kresha shook her head. "No—what are we doing?" She grinned. "See how better I am getting?"

"You're doing great," Lily said. "Okay—now here's the deal."

Talking as fast as she could, with one eye on her watch, Lily filled Kresha in on her plan. She watched her carefully, but Kresha never wavered, never questioned. When Lily was finished, she repeated it all back—Kresha style.

"Ve only vork on tings ve know—we know—are not fair. Ve start vit—with the clothes."

"And don't forget that you and I will be together as often as we can, so Deputy Dog will see us."

"But we don't—vhat vas vord?"

"We don't taunt her—you know—throw it in her face that we're following all the rules."

"Goot. Got it!" Kresha grinned and nodded at Lily's shirt. "I vant shirt like yours."

"We need to make a bunch of shirts," Lily said. "Can you come over this afternoon?"

Kresha nodded happily. As Lily hurried to third period, she started to sag again. She had imagined *all* the Girlz making shirts together. It was sad to think of just her and Kresha.

But it's not gonna be that way forever, she told herself firmly. *It won't be long before they'll see it our way.*

The day wasn't as hard to get through as she thought it would be. In third and fourth periods, it hurt to see Reni and Suzy sitting together and passing Girlz-Grams she'd never get to see. But as soon as she finished her assignments, she wrote a Gram to Kresha, and that made it better.

At lunch, Reni, Suzy and Zooey looked fragile as they sat at the now half-empty Girlz table. Lily's chest ached when she glanced at her used-to-be chair, so she stopped looking in their direction and concentrated on sharing her carrot sticks with Kresha and planning their T-shirts.

Then seventh period came.

Mr. Nutting was giving a test, and for once the room was perfectly silent except for the rubbing of erasers as people had second thoughts about their answers. It was Kresha's first test in a regular class, and Lily was a little worried. She glanced over to see if Kresha was erasing as much as everyone else.

But Kresha was writing busily, frowning once, and then grinning at the paper and putting down an answer. She seemed to sense Lily looking at her, because she looked up.

Are you okay? Lily said with her eyes. She gave Kresha a thumbs-up.

Kresha nodded, grinning, and gave a thumbs-up back.

"What's going on here?" Mr. Nutting said.

Lily's head jerked up. He was standing behind her, arms folded, one hand tugging on his beard. There was an accusation in his eyes.

"Excuse me?" Lily said.

"What's all this?" He put his thumb up, then put it down, then put it up again, all the time smiling stupidly. The smile faded. "Some kind of sign language?"

By now other students were stirring in their seats. Out of the corner of her eye, Lily could see Reni watching her. Lily tilted up her chin.

"No," she said. "I was just concerned about her, so I signaled if she was okay. She said yes. That's all."

Her voice sounded even and clear, not a trace of fear in it. It gave her more courage.

"She is not your concern," Mr. Nutting said. "*You* are your concern. And mine." He beckoned at her with his hand. "Let me see your paper."

"I'm not finished yet," Lily said.

"You might be. Let me have it."

Lily handed it to him and watched as his eyes ran down the page. Her heart didn't pound. Her face didn't get blotchy. So what if her hands got a little sweaty? He didn't have to know that.

As he read her test, Lily glanced over at Kresha. She looked confused. Ever so slightly, Lily shook her head. Then she demonstrated tilting up her chin and straightening her shoulders. Kresha imitated her. Lily smiled.

Mr. Nutting looked up from the paper and held out his hand to Kresha. "Let me see yours."

At this point, everybody was looking. Suzy was white-faced. Benjamin and Bernadette were on the edges of their seats, watching in fascination. Ashley and Chelsea were snickering. Marcie McCleary was using this opportunity to look at Reni's paper.

"This is pretty much what I expected," Mr. Nutting said. He snapped Kresha's paper up against Lily's and jerked his head toward the door. "Come with me, both of you."

A low murmur went through the room.

"The rest of you get back to work. I'll be watching."

Kresha looked at Lily with a flash of fear in her eyes.

We haven't done anything wrong, Lily told her with hers.

Okay, Kresha answered back.

They both followed Mr. Nutting out into the hall, where he stationed himself so he could continue to monitor the class. If anybody was concentrating on the test, Lily couldn't see how. Heads were coming up every few seconds to crane for a glimpse of Lily and Kresha getting busted.

"We weren't cheating, Mr. Nutting," Lily said, head still high.

"Really? Then how do you account for the fact that at this point, you have given similar answers to every question?"

"You think we were exchanging answers?" Lily said.

"I think you were giving *her* answers, yes."

"But how would I do that?"

"I don't know. Suppose you tell me."

"I can't, because I didn't."

"She did not," Kresha said. "I know answers myself." She gave a strong nod that made Lily proud.

"Even though you've only been in this class a week," Mr. Nutting said, disbelief etched in his face.

"Ya. I study. Hard."

"Uh-huh."

Something about the way he said it set the porcupine quills on end. *This is it,* Lily thought. *This is why I'm an advocate. It's time to do what Art said.*

Lily cleared her throat and pointed to the front of her shirt. "Do you know what this means, Mr. Nutting?"

Mr. Nutting glanced at it and smirked. "I'll be over later? No—of course I know what it means. What's your point?"

"We—Kresha and I—are trying to overcome injustice in this school. And this is injustice. You automatically think that just because Kresha comes from another country, she's not as smart as we are and can't make an A on one of your tests." Lily gave her head a final nod—sending red hair sprawling across her face. She made a note to herself to do something about that—and Kresha's bangs too.

"All right," Mr. Nutting said. "Tell you what I'll do. I'm going to bring a desk out here and have Kresha take the rest of her test in the hall, with her back to you. I'm going to turn your desk around too, so that there is no possible way you can look at each other. How's that?"

"You can do that, can't you Kresha?" Lily said.

Kresha said, "Yes. I can do that. I can do it standing on my head if you vant."

"No, I don't 'vant'—and don't you two get smart with me."

"She was just trying to make a point," Lily said.

"So am I. Now go."

Lily tried not to grin too broadly as she went back into the room, turned her desk around, and started in on her test again. Her writing looked a little wiggly now because her hand was shaking some, but she decided that was from excitement.

When she finished, she glanced up. Reni was looking at her.

Lily smiled. *Do you see how it works?* she said with her eyes.

Reni's eyes didn't say anything. Then she shook her head—frowned—and went back to her test.

Chapter 11

It's just going to take more time, that's all," Lily told Kresha that afternoon as they were working on their T-shirts in Lily's kitchen.

"You think tomorrow?" Kresha asked.

"I don't know." Lily paused with a tube of pink fabric paint in her hand. "But I know Reni. We're gonna have to do something big before she'll change her mind."

Kresha shook her bangs out of her eyes. "Reni only?"

"If we get Reni, we'll get Suzy and Zooey too. And Kresh?"

"Ya?"

"We have to do something about our hair. The opponent has to be able to see our eyes."

"What is opponent?" Kresha said.

"That's what I'd like to know," Mom said.

She was standing in the doorway with the usual bags of groceries in her arms. She didn't look happy. In fact, her mouth hadn't twitched toward a smile since about halftime at yesterday's game—at least not at Lily.

Mom headed for the counter with the groceries. "Please tell me you're going to be in a chess tournament or something."

"I don't play chess," Lily said. She was careful to keep the edge out of her voice.

"Then who's this 'opponent'? And hi, Kresha. How are you, Hon?"

"No good, Missa Robbinz," Kresha said sadly. "Lily and me—we have hard fight."

Kresha, would you shush! Lily tried to say with her eyes.

"Really?" Mom said. "What kind of fight?"

"Fight for justice," Kresha said. She held up her partially painted, black shirt.

"'Student Pow'?" Mom said. She looked at Lily.

"'Student Power,'" Lily said.

"Those are definitely fighting words," Mom said. "It would get *my* dander up if a student walked in wearing that." She leaned against the sink, arms folded, groceries forgotten. There wasn't a twitch within a hundred miles. "It's really interesting," Mom went on. "I kind of like to think the teachers and the students are on the same side. Now, if you wore a shirt saying 'Education Power' or 'Mighty School,' I'd have you make one for *me*."

"You not—do not vant von like these?" Kresha said.

"No, Kresha," Mom said. "I don't."

She still didn't take her eyes off Lily, and Lily was certain that any second she'd be ordered to toss shirts—paint and all—right into the trash can. She also expected her hackles to stand up, but her chest ached instead.

Mom chewed at her lower lip for a minute, and then she turned to the groceries. "As soon as you're finished, Lil, you'll have to clean that up and set the table. Staying for supper, Kresha?"

Kresha did stay, and they did get their T-shirts painted and had them drying on the shower rod in the spare bathroom before Kresha went home. It gave Lily time to prepare for the lecture she was sure to get the minute her friend went out the front door.

When Mom and Dad both came to her room, they looked so grim that Otto retreated under the bed without growling. Lily tried to stiffen herself up.

"Your mom says you and Kresha seem to be taking a stand at school," Dad said.

"Yeah," Lily said. "But it's only about stuff that's totally unfair—"

Dad put his hand up. "Before you go any further, hear us out."

"Okay," Lily said. *Here it comes. Please, God, don't let them make me stop!*

"We think you need some guidelines for whatever it is you're doing," Dad said.

"If you'd just let me *tell* you what we're doing—"

"I'd rather tell you what we expect and let you decide whether what you're up to is right or not," he said.

Lily couldn't help gaping at him. "You would?" she said.

"You sound surprised," Mom said. "Haven't we always treated you with respect? Given you the benefit of the doubt?"

"Um—I guess," Lily said.

"Which is more than I can say for your attitude toward us lately," she said.

Dad put his hand on her arm. They had one of those silent parent conversations, and Mom pressed her lips together.

"So," Dad said, looking at Mom, "except for a little display of 'attitude' lately, you've given us no reason to do otherwise. We're going to continue to respect and trust you. Fair enough?"

"Okay," Lily said. This wasn't at all what she expected, and her heart was suddenly racing. *Stop!* she told it. *What's your problem?*

"All right," Dad said. He settled himself on the edge of Lily's desk. Mom leaned against the doorframe. "Number one: you are not to disobey any rules—no matter how silly you may think they are."

"I'm not!" Lily said.

"Good. Number two: you are not to treat any person in authority any differently than you would your mother or me."

Mom cleared her throat.

"Let me elaborate," Dad said. "No disrespect. Clear enough?"

"I never do," Lily said. "Even though sometimes they deserve it."

"Don't push it, Lil," Mom said.

Her eyes were so stern, Lily pressed *her* lips together.

"Number three:" Dad went on. "You are to be very careful about your reputation."

"What's a reputation?" Lily said.

"In twenty-five words or less," Mom said to Dad.

"It's what other people in general think of you."

"But that's just the point!" Lily said. "I don't *care* what other people think of me, as long as I stand up for what's right!"

Dad looked at her for what seemed like a long time, and Lily couldn't look away. This wasn't the vague, "my mind is a thousand miles away with C.S. Lewis" father she was used to dealing with. He was talking to her as if a lot depended on her understanding every word he said.

Finally, he continued, "We just want you to be very, *very* sure that you're ready for whatever consequences there may be."

"If you mean, like, getting detention or something, they can't do that if we're not breaking any rules."

"I'm talking about the people who have a good opinion of you changing their minds."

"Well, Mr. Nutting never liked me anyway, so—"

"What about your friends?" Mom said. "Why was Kresha the only one over here this afternoon?"

That one Lily couldn't answer—not because she didn't know, but because she was afraid to talk. She knew tears weren't that far away.

"Just think about it," Dad said. "Pray about it. If you want to talk to us, we're available." He glanced at Mom. "But we're going to respect your right to decide for yourself."

There was a fleeting moment where Lily wanted to cry out, *No! Don't let me do this! I'm scared!*

But that moment evaporated so quickly, Lily wasn't sure it had been there at all. She could do this. She could follow their guidelines— at least the first two. And that thing about reputation—she *was* ready for the consequences. Everybody was going to respect her once she and Kresha showed them they couldn't be walked on. And the Girlz were going to be the first ones to change their minds.

"You don't want to say anything?"

Lily looked up at Dad. He was still wearing that concerned expression.

"No," Lily said. "But thanks for coming by. I'll follow the guidelines, I promise."

Dad looked at Mom. She scratched under her nose and said, "Okay. The offer's always open. We're here."

"Okay," Lily said, and went to check on the T-shirts.

She and Kresha wore them the next day, and by the end of the day, Lily was convinced they'd scored a number of little victories.

Before school, they sat together on the bench, "Student Power" shirts plainly in view when Deputy Dog came by to patrol the area. She stopped, appeared to read them, and then just shook her head and walked on. But she seemed to be everywhere the rest of the morning, watching Lily from corners and doorways. She even strolled through the library when Lily was renewing her book on Gandhi.

"Overdue book?" Officer Horn said to the librarian.

"No," she said, still tapping away at the computer keys. "Lily never turns a book in late. In fact, she's renewing this one two days before she has to."

Lily smiled sweetly at Deputy Dog.

It wasn't quite that simple just before third period when Lily was loitering outside Mrs. Reinhold's door, just to give Reni a chance to say hi to her. She'd calculated exactly how long it would take her to get to her seat a fraction of a second before the bell rang, and she still had eighty-five seconds to spare when Deputy Dog prowled down the hall.

"All right, Robbins, let's get to class," she said in a too-loud voice.

Lily smiled at Officer Horn and said, "I'm waiting for somebody. I still have time."

"What is it with you?" Deputy Dog said. "What—you have to push everything right to the limit?"

Lily glanced at her watch. Sixty-five seconds. "Am I disturbing somebody by standing here?" she asked. "If I am, I'll be glad to move on."

"You really think you are 'it' on a stick, don't you?" Officer Horn said. "And yes, as a matter of fact, you're disturbing *me*."

Lily was relieved when her hackles began to stand up. That always helped. "How?" she said, careful to keep her voice polite.

"By flaunting that shirt, for openers," Officer Horn said. "And don't tell me you're expressing yourself. The only thing you're telling me is that you have an attitude bigger than Philadelphia!"

Lily didn't hear the rest of what she said because Reni was just then entering Mrs. Reinhold's room. She looked over her shoulder, and Lily held her breath. But it wasn't respect she saw in Reni's eyes. It was that same concern thing she'd seen in Dad's.

Lily pushed away the ache in her chest and looked at her watch. "I'm sorry, Officer Horn," she said, "I have to get to my seat. Mrs. Reinhold doesn't like us to be late."

"Oh, my," Officer Horn said. "You don't question that rule?"

"No," Lily said. "Because *that* rule makes sense. May I go now?"

"Go," Officer Horn said. But her muddy-brown eyes didn't have respect in them either. She just looked disgusted.

Still, after getting through lunch without another conversation with Officer Horn and getting an A on Mr. Nutting's test—*and* finding out that Kresha had gotten one too—she declared to Kresha as they walked to their lockers together that it had been a successful day.

"But, Lily," Kresha said. "Reni and Suzy and Zooey—they still no—vill not—talk to me."

"We have to give it time," Lily said.

"I miss them," Kresha said.

Lily sighed. "That's one of the sacrifices we have to make to stand up for our rights."

"Okay," Kresha said.

Lily wasn't sure her voice was as enthusiastic as it had been the day before. She was about to say, *You're still in this with me, aren't you, Kresh?* when they rounded the corner to the locker area and saw Suzy and Zooey just a few feet away.

Lily pulled Kresha into the next row of lockers until the Girlz passed. When they were gone, Kresha pointed to the ground.

"Look, Lily," she said. "They drop a Gram."

Lily scooped it up.

"I give it to them?" Kresha said.

"I guess we should," Lily said. "I'll stick it in whoever's locker it is."

But she wasn't sure Kresha heard her. Kresha was staring after Suzy and Zooey like a puppy who'd just been left behind at the pound.

I miss them too, Lily thought. She missed giggling with them on the phone. She missed trading cookies with them at lunch. She looked down at the Girlz-Gram in her hand. She missed getting notes from them.

Before she even thought about whether it was right or not, she opened the Gram that hadn't been written to her. It was to Suzy—from Reni.

"Scared about my audition today," Reni had written in clipped, Girlz-Gram style. "Will die if I don't make it."

I'll die if you don't either, Lily thought.

And then an urge washed over her like a giant wave—the urge to run to the orchestra room and find Reni and tell her to please forget passive resistance and causes and all that stuff . . . the urge to grab her and all the Girlz by the hands and pray together until Reni blew all those committee people away with the way she played the violin. Maybe praying with the Girlz was what she missed the most.

She suddenly felt something brush her cheek. It was Kresha's hand.

"Don't cry, Lily," she said. "Maybe tomorrow, ya?"

Lily smacked at the tear. "Yeah," she said. "Come on—let's go in the bathroom and work on our hair. I've been meaning for us to do that and I keep forgetting."

Fifteen minutes of slicking back their hair not only left them looking like they were made of tougher stuff but also took away some of the ache in Lily's chest.

"Use some hair spray or gel or something tomorrow morning," Lily said before Kresha hurried off to catch her bus, her stubborn bangs already falling back down over her forehead. Lily took one more look at herself in the mirror.

Now they're gonna know I'm serious about this, she thought. But that thought didn't stick. Her mind raced back to Reni. Right now she was probably playing her violin for a committee of stony-faced people who were going to determine whether Reni "lived or died."

"I should be there with her," Lily said to the strange-looking girl in the mirror—the tough-looking girl who looked like she could never cry but was sobbing her heart out.

From outside the door, she heard voices, and grabbing her backpack, she dove into one of the stalls. She closed the door just as the hall door opened on a girl's voice. It sounded like Bernadette, talking in the voice she used for people in her "group."

"And did you see that shirt she was wearing today?"

"Yeah—her friend was wearing one just like it—you know, that foreign chick."

"I thought it was cool when she helped me and Benjamin, but now she's, like, getting all weird."

"Uh—ye-ah! I wouldn't wear some lame homemade shirt if you paid me."

"Aw, man, there's no toilet paper in here—you got any on your side?"

"Yeah—I'll pass it under."

Lily grabbed her backpack off the hook and tiptoed out of the stall, barely able to see for the tears.

"Was somebody in here?" she heard Bernadette say.

With the bathroom door still closing behind her, Lily slung her pack on and went for the corner at a dead run, tears now dripping off her chin. But suddenly, from out of some crack in the wall it seemed, a figure stepped into her path. It was Officer Horn.

"Oops, Robbins," she said. "You picked the wrong rule to push this time. There is absolutely *no* running in these halls."

Lily screeched to a halt. Her heart felt as if it were all the way up in her throat. "I'm sorry," she managed to say around it. "I'll slow down—I was just trying to catch my bus."

"I'd have accepted that a week ago—before I knew you."

"Please," Lily said. "I'm sorry—I was just upset about my friend."

"Look, you had your chance with me and you blew it." Officer Horn had her thumbs hooked on her belt in the usual way, but there was something very different in her voice. It wasn't sarcastic anymore.

"I wasn't pushing this time," Lily said. "Honest, you have to believe me. I was upset about my friend—and then these girls came in the bathroom, and they were talking about me—I'm so—"

"Me too, Robbins," Officer Horn said. She put her hand around Lily's arm. "I really am. I thought you'd get the message before and you didn't. Now you've left me no choice. Come on, let's take a little walk to the office."

Lily started to cry in earnest now, and she didn't care that she sounded like Zooey. Even when out of the corner of her eye she saw Bernadette passing, staring openly, she didn't care about that either. This wasn't the way she'd envisioned herself going to the office— because this wasn't about the cause.

"I'd advise you not to make an issue out of it," Officer Horn was saying in that new voice. "Just come with me."

"Why don't I save you the trouble?" another voice said.

This one belonged to Mr. Miniver. And his sounded different too. It sounded very, very disappointed.

Chapter 12

Disappointed or not, it was a voice Lily was glad to hear. She wanted to throw her arms around Mr. Miniver.

"No offense, Mr. Miniver," Officer Horn said, "but I think I better handle this."

"Normally I'd say go right ahead," Mr. Miniver said. "I think we both feel a little let down by Lily right now. But there are some extenuating circumstances." He looked at Lily. "Would you just stand over there for a minute and let me have a word with Officer Horn?"

Lily nodded miserably and moved down the hall, planting herself against the wall. The thought of taking off running passed through her head, but what would be the point? Wherever she went, nobody would understand.

She couldn't even feel relieved when Officer Horn disappeared down the hall. When Mr. Miniver joined Lily, he still looked disappointed, but there was something else on his face too. He was so serious that it scared her.

"I'm not going to lecture you," he said. "You're upset enough as it is. I guess I didn't get to you soon enough, did I? Who told you?"

"Told me what?" Lily said. "Did something happen?"

"Yeah, Lily-Pad, it did. Reni didn't make All-State Orchestra."

Lily stared at him. "But she had to! She worked so hard!"

"I knew you'd be upset—that's why I came looking for you as soon as Mr. Lamb told me. Of course, she's heartbroken."

"It's my fault!" Lily said. She was crying harder than ever. "I made her upset before the audition—and I wasn't there to pray with her— I've messed up everything, and that wasn't what I meant to do at all."

"Lily," Mr. Miniver said. He put his hands on her shoulders. "Everything isn't up to you. There are some things you just can't control—and this is one of them."

"Then, what happened?" Lily said. "She's good—even Mr. Lamb said so!"

Mr. Miniver shook his head. "Sometimes there are factors we can't account for. Do you want to see Reni?"

"Where is she?" Lily said.

"She's in Mr. Lamb's office. I was on my way down there. He says she's pretty upset, but I thought maybe you might want to talk to her first, as close as you two are."

Lily started to take off like a shot, but Mr. Miniver took hold of her backpack.

"Don't run," he said. He glanced over his shoulder. "You sure know how to get the law on your trail."

But Lily didn't give Officer Horn a second thought. She didn't even think about whether Reni would tell her to go away the minute she walked in the door. She just walked as fast as she dared until she got to the music hall.

She'd been there before, waiting for Reni to finish practicing, and she knew Mr. Lamb's office was just off the orchestra room. She had her hand on the door when she saw the sign on it: *Auditions in Progress. Please Do Not Disturb.*

She stood on her toes and peered through the window. There were no auditions going on at the moment. There were only three people, two women and a man, sitting at a table in the back, sipping from throwaway cups. Lily didn't recognize them, but decided they must be part of the committee.

Lily was about to shove through the door when she realized that the voices coming from the back of the room were slightly raised. It didn't sound like a conversation she wanted to walk in on. Impatiently, she leaned against the door and waited for them finish so she could get to Reni.

The voices drifted out to the hall. "I think we ought to reconsider that little black girl," one of the women said.

"Like I told you, they never stick to anything," the man said. "We had two blacks last year, and they both dropped out and left us with big holes."

"She was the best one we heard today."

"It wasn't the style we're after. Lamb ought to put her in a jazz band. They're good at that."

"You better watch it, Hal. You're bordering on racism. Somebody'll be screaming discrimination."

"I'll tell 'somebody' what I'm telling you—we have to consider more than good playing. Does the student stay with things—have decent self-discipline? They can't argue with that."

I can! Lily wanted to scream through the door. *Reni practices everyday! I hardly get to see her, she practices so much—*

And then it hit her as if they'd thrown a violin case at her. That judge wasn't letting Reni into All-State—because she was black.

Inside the orchestra room, chairs scraped back, and through the window, Lily could see them tucking their papers into their briefcases. She retreated to the water fountain until they'd left. Then she rammed through the door, took the room at a pace that violated Deputy Dog's no-running rule four times over, and burst into Mr. Lamb's office.

Reni was there alone, head on her arms on the desk, shoulders shaking. When she looked up, she said, "Oh, Lily! I didn't make it!"

"I know," Lily said.

And then Reni was standing up and they were hugging and crying together. They didn't let go until Reni said, "I need to blow my nose. I'm getting snot all over your shirt."

"It's a stupid shirt anyway," Lily said. "I'm gonna burn it. This is all my fault, Reni."

Reni shook her head as she honked into a tissue. "It wasn't you. I played so good, Lily. I played the best I ever did! Even Mr. Lamb said so." She shrugged. "I guess there were a lot of other people who were better. I was like the last one they heard. I thought that would be a good thing, but I guess it wasn't."

Lily opened her mouth to tell her the real reason. But Reni put her arms around Lily again and cried and hiccuped until Lily was sure Reni would throw up. If Lily told her now what she knew, she was likely to do that.

"I need my mom," Reni said. "Would you call her to come get me?"

"Sure," Lily said.

"She could—she could take you home—too."

But Lily shook her head. "I still have stuff to do here."

A plan was already taking shape in Lily's head—and none of it had anything to do with T-shirts or hairdos or passive resistance.

All Reni's teachers know she has self-discipline, Lily thought as she helped Reni with her backpack and got her to the door. *And I bet a bunch of them are still here. I could get their sworn statements today.*

Mr. Miniver arrived to take over with Reni, and Mr. Lamb went with them. Lily would have to fill him in later. She kissed Reni on the forehead and took off for Ms. Bavetta's room. Being a music teacher, she was in this wing. She'd be easy to convince too, Lily was sure.

Ms. Bavetta, carrying two tote bags bulging with student papers, was just closing her classroom door when Lily charged up to her.

"Ms Bavetta!" she said, breathing like a locomotive. "I need your help. Reni Johnson didn't get picked for All-State Orchestra because she's black, and this one judge thinks she won't be disciplined enough because of that, and that's, like, so unfair, and I need you to write a statement for Reni saying what a good student she is and all—I mean, would you?"

Ms. Bavetta dug into one of the bags. "Where did I put my keys this time?" she said.

Lily wanted to stomp her foot and scream, *Listen to me!* Instead, she said, "Would you? Like, before you leave?"

"I'm sorry to hear that about Reni," Ms. Bavetta said, still digging. "She's a nice girl. But frankly, I don't think your coming to her rescue is the best idea I've ever heard."

"But that judge is being so unfair! That's discrimination!"

"You say that about seating charts, Lily," Ms. Bavetta said. She produced a wad of keys and began flipping through them. "I don't think I want to be involved in your 'Student Power' thing." She jabbed one of the keys into the lock and gave it a wrench. "I have to go," she said.

Lily stared after Ms. Bavetta as she and her perfume faded down the hall. Lily screamed after her in her mind—*But this is* important! *This isn't like seating charts! This isn't* about *Student Power! This is like Martin Luther King or something!*

But she didn't have time to waste arguing. With her hackles standing right up on end, she headed for Mr. Nutting's room. He was sitting with his feet up on his desk, grading papers when she burst in and gave him the same speech she'd delivered to Ms. Bavetta. When he slowly pulled his legs off the desktop, Lily felt some hope.

"Which one is Reni?" he said.

Lily pulled her hands into fists at her sides. "She's the only black girl in our class. And that's just it—she's being discriminated against!"

"You sure get yourself tangled up in other people's business, don't you, Red?" he said. "First it was the Croatian kid. Now it's the African. You're running out of minorities."

"No!" Lily said. "It's not like that! This is for real!"

"Yeah, but my question is—is that hairdo for real?"

Lily didn't even answer him. She stormed out of the room, hot from scalp to toenails, and went for Mrs. Reinhold's room. She might be old-fashioned, but at least she was fair.

The English teacher was busy straightening the desks, but she stopped when Lily said from the doorway, "Mrs. Reinhold, I need your help."

"What on earth, Lilianna?" she said. "You look wretched, child!"

She hurried over to Lily the way her grandmother would have, and it nearly reduced Lily to tears. But she had to stay strong. This was about Reni.

Mrs. Reinhold made her sit down and offered to fix her a cup of tea, but Lily shook her head and launched once more into her tirade.

"Are you absolutely sure of what you heard?" Mrs. Reinhold said.

"Yes! But nobody will believe me. I knew *you* would, though. If you would write a statement about Reni right now, I could—"

Lily stopped. Mrs. Reinhold was slowly shaking her head.

"Why not?" Lily said.

"Probably for the same reason none of the other teachers would," she said. She adjusted her tiny glasses with her index fingers and looked down her pointy nose at Lily. "We all would have jumped to help the old Lily, no questions asked. At least I would have. But this Lily we know now—we'd be insane to take her at her word. She runs around smart-mouthing teachers, putting them off with her attire— now she's resorted to some rebel hairstyle—"

"Forget my hair!" Lily cried.

"I beg your pardon?"

"I'm sorry—I'm just so mad. Mrs. Reinhold—I never did any of those things in your class. I treat you with respect."

"You don't think word gets around, Lilianna? You don't think we discuss things in the faculty lounge? A lot of it is gossip, and I don't listen to that. But when every one of your teachers comments about your attitude, I tend to pay attention. We *all* pay attention. It's no wonder nobody will listen to you anymore."

"But it isn't about me!" Lily said. "It's about Reni."

"What is? Something you *think* you heard? Something you may very well have blown out of proportion in that amazing imagination of yours? I can't fly off the handle and throw some recommendation in a colleague's face just on the basis of a claim by a student who jumps at every safe chance to defy authority." She adjusted the glasses again. "I try to protect my reputation, Lilianna," she said. "I suggest you start doing the same. I want to have the *old* Lily back."

Why was it that no one, absolutely no one, understood what she was trying to do? Lily muttered a thank-you and shuffled out of the room, dragging her backpack behind her. There were no porcupine quills now. All she felt was despair.

She'd even missed the late bus. It was already pulling out of the circular drive when Lily got to the front of the school. She sank wearily onto a bench.

But no sooner had her seat touched the wood than she heard a voice behind her. Deputy Dog.

"What are you still doing on the school grounds, Robbins?" she said.

"I missed the bus," Lily said woodenly.

"So what's your plan?"

"My plan? My plan didn't work. I don't know what I'm going to do now."

Officer Horn put her foot up on the bench. "I'm talking about your plan for getting home."

"I don't have one," Lily said. She was so sad, all she could do was watch the bus disappear and wish she could do the same.

"I've got one for you," Officer Horn said. "And I suggest you follow it before you get yourself in real trouble. Mr. Miniver said you were upset—what else is new—but you can't do anything for your friend. She's suffering from life. It's full of disappointment. So I suggest you either call your mom on that pay phone over there or you start walking. But if you hang around campus a minute longer, I *am* gonna haul you in. Understood?"

Mom, Lily thought. *I need Mom.*

"Okay," Lily said. "I'll walk."

She could feel Officer Horn watching her as she struggled off down the sidewalk toward the high school as if, Lily thought, she'd just been ordered out of a store for suspicion of shoplifting. But Lily didn't turn around to see. She just kept her eyes on getting to where Mom was.

When she got to the high school gym, Mom had her whole volleyball team sitting on the gym floor with her. They were laughing, obviously about something Mom had just said because her mouth was twitching in the nearest thing to a smile.

"Hey, Coach," somebody said. "Isn't that your daughter?"

Mom looked up at Lily, and the twitching stopped. She gave a soft toot on her whistle. "Okay, start your laps," she said. "I'll make announcements later."

Mom stood up, and Lily dumped her backpack on the floor and ran to her. Mom held her arms out and enfolded them around Lily so tightly that Lily didn't even have to stand on her own feet. She sagged against her mother and cried it all out—every detail—from what she heard the judges say to Officer Horn ordering her off the middle-school campus.

"I can't do it anymore, Mom," Lily said as she was winding down. "I thought I could be this 'advocate' and fight for things like Gandhi and Martin Luther King, but I can't. I blew the whole thing, and now I have to quit."

Mom held Lily away at arm's length. Her brown eyes were shining.

"Quit?" she said. "Oh, no, Lil, there will be no quitting now." She shook her head until her ponytail swayed. "You can't quit now. You finally have something worth fighting for."

Chapter
13

"But, Mom—" Lily said. "I don't see how—"

"Stick with me, Lil," Mom said. She winked at her. "I'm going to show you how this is done."

She made Lily go into the coaches' bathroom and wash her face while she made some phone calls. When Lily came out, tears gone and hair back to its normal state, Mom had already dismissed the team and had her purse over her shoulder.

"Dad's going to meet us at home," Mom said. "So is Art. Joe's going to Trent's for the evening. I don't think we need his input."

Lily had to run to keep up with her as they headed for the parking lot. She found herself looking back over her shoulder for Officer Horn.

"What are we going to do at home?" Lily said.

"Eat the pizza I ordered," Mom said. "And then pray."

Dad, Art, and the pizza delivery boy all arrived about the same time. Dad and Mom conferred in the kitchen while Art got out napkins and paper plates. He set them on the coffee table in the living room next to two legal pads and several sharpened pencils Mom had put there.

"Dude, we're mobilizing," Art said. "What did you get into, kid?"

"Tell me too," Dad said from the doorway. "Start from the beginning."

Once again, Lily told her story. When she got to the part about the judge saying "they" never stuck to anything, Art gave a low whistle.

"You're absolutely sure that's what he said?" Dad asked Lily.

"That's exactly what I heard," Lily said. "I wouldn't make up something like that. Honest, Dad."

"That's all I needed to hear," Dad said. He put out both hands. Mom grabbed onto one, and Lily took the other. Art put his palm in hers on the other side. When he gave it a squeeze, she started to cry.

She cried all through Dad praying for Jesus to be their advocate and Reni's ... through Mom asking the Holy Spirit to give them all strength and courage and wisdom ... and especially through Art asking God to forgive him for giving Lily crummy advice.

When they raised their heads, Dad said, "I think we better get the Johnsons over here."

Mom had the pizza reheated when Reni and her parents arrived, but nobody ate any. They seemed to lose their appetites as Dad gave them the *Reader's Digest* version of Lily's story.

"It's up to you," Dad said to Mr. and Mrs. Johnson. "But if it were my daughter, I'd ask for an investigation. If you decide to do that, we'll help all we can."

"Are there legal channels we should go through?" Mr. Johnson asked.

Legal channels? Reni said to Lily with her eyes.

Lily at once imagined herself on the witness stand, hair pulled back so the prosecuting attorney could see the honesty and bravery in her eyes. But she turned a mental hose on that image and washed it away. This wasn't about her anymore. It never should have been.

It'll be okay, Lily told Reni with *her* eyes. *My mom and dad know exactly what they're doing.*

"I think you start by talking to Mr. Lamb, then the school administration," Dad was saying. "But if you want legal counsel before you even start, we have an excellent attorney."

Mom leaned over and put her lips close to Lily's ear. "This is going to get pretty boring," she whispered. "Why don't you and Reni go into the kitchen and get yourselves something to drink. We'll call you when we need you."

Lily motioned Reni into the kitchen with her head, and Reni seemed more than happy to leave the family room with all the talk about a lawyer. But Lily was nervous. Except for Reni hiccupping into her shoulder that afternoon, Reni hadn't spoken to her in days.

But I have to talk to her, Lily told herself.

"I could probably help you more," she said as Reni hiked herself up to sit on the counter and Lily dug through the pantry for cans of soda, "but I've messed up my reputation with all our teachers so none of them will listen to me. I was thinking they could write statements for you—but they wouldn't write me a bathroom pass now, I bet. None of them even believed me, I know that."

She pulled her head out, 7 UPs in hand. Reni was watching her.

"That's because they don't really know you," Reni said. "Like right now, I can tell you're not just trying to do some big thing. I can tell you're, like, totally sincere."

"Then I don't care if no teacher ever believes a single thing I say, ever again," Lily said. "As long as you do."

"Girls," Mom called from the family room. "We need you."

"I'll do anything to help," Lily said to Reni. "No matter what it is."

"Girls," Dad said to them. "We all agree that the best thing you can do is say absolutely nothing to anyone at school about any of this. Rumors get started, and then they get out of control. All that would do is hurt Reni's case."

Reni and Lily both nodded. Mom's lips twitched in Lily's direction.

"You sure, Lil? I mean, asking you to do nothing is like asking anybody else to sacrifice a kidney or something."

Lily waited for the porcupine quills, but none came. In fact, she smiled at her mom. "I can keep my mouth shut," she said.

Nobody looked terribly convinced. Dad put his arm around her. "Just in case, though, Liliputian," he said, "I'd pray about that, if I were you."

Lily did, that same night. Propped against China, with Otto at her side taking the fuzz off yet another tennis ball, Lily started to write in her journal.

"Lord, Dad said you're the advocate, Jesus. Mr. Miniver told me that too—"

She stopped writing and gnawed on her pen. Otto turned from the tennis ball and eyed it enviously.

Mr. Miniver had told her to look up the advocate thing in the Bible, but she'd never done it. She pawed around on her bedside table and found her Bible under a pile of fabric paints and old T-shirts yet to be lettered with protests. She made a note to get rid of those later.

She thumbed through the pages until Mr. Miniver's words came back to her. "Try reading 1 John 2," he had said. Lily found it and started to read: "If anybody does sin, we have one who speaks to the Father in our defense—Jesus Christ, the Righteous One."

He'd also said to read about Jesus—the advocate—sticking up for people. That thing about throwing stones—she found it in the gospel of John in chapter 8.

As she closed the book, Lily's neck was prickly, but it wasn't because of Mr. Miniver, Dad, or even the Bible for reminding her. Every inch of prickly skin was poking right back at her.

"I should have believed it sooner," she wrote in her journal. "I should have known it was *my* voice I was hearing and not yours. I was being a show-off again. I'm going to make sure from now on—I promise."

She closed her eyes. There was a peaceful thought—this time, at last, she was standing up for the *right* rights. And then, still "standing up," she fell asleep.

The next several days weren't easy. It was even harder than Lily had expected to do absolutely nothing to help Reni. But at least there were other things to think about.

There were teachers to apologize to. Ms. Bavetta and Mr. Nutting didn't seem to know what to make of it. Mrs. Reinhold, however, gave a satisfied nod and said, "It's good to have you back, Lilianna." Then she said, "How did things work out for Reni?"

Lily chewed at her lip for a moment, and then she said, "We don't know yet."

"No protest march? No shaved head?" Mrs. Reinhold said. But she was closer to a smile than Lily had seen her in a long time. She was reminding Lily more of her mom all the time.

That was the other thing that needed to be taken care of while she waited for things to happen for Reni. She had to make up with Mom.

When she told Mom she wanted to talk to her, Mom suggested they go shopping on Saturday and then grab some lunch.

"But you hate to shop!" Lily said.

"Right—just like you hate football. But, Lil, just because we don't like the same things doesn't mean we can't be close. I can compromise—we'll shop for sports bras or something."

"Mo-om!"

"Just kidding, Lil. Just kidding."

They settled for lunch at their favorite diner on Route 130. Lily ordered double mashed potatoes with gravy and made her apology to Mom while they waited and sucked down chocolate milk shakes.

"I've been a real creep to you lately, and I'm sorry," Lily said, staring at her straw. "I don't know what was up with me—I'd just get so annoyed with everything you said—but I'm not gonna feel that way ever again. You and Dad are the best."

"I appreciate the sentiment, Lil," Mom said, "But you will get irritated with us at least a hundred more times before you reach the old age of twenty-five and realize we've suddenly gotten smarter."

"Nuh-uh!"

"Yuh-huh! It's a normal part of growing up."

Lily shook her head. "I got in trouble being normal."

"No—you got in trouble doing the wrong thing with being normal."

"That's what Mr. Miniver says. Sometimes I get so confused about what the right thing is."

"That's why you have God."

"I know—and I'm doing a lot better about, like, not telling *him* what to do."

"That's big of you," Mom said.

"And I'm not gonna get so carried away with stuff from now on."

Mom stuck her straw back in her milk shake and gave Lily a serious look. "Don't say that, Lil," she said. "Your passion is so much a part of who you are. You'll learn to channel it—but don't try to teach yourself not to have it. You'd be squelching the best part of yourself."

"Yeah, but people think I'm weird when I do stuff."

"What people?"

"Like Bernadette—"

"Who?"

"She's this girl—"

"Do you respect her opinion?"

Lily only had to think about it for a few seconds. "No," she said. "I guess I don't."

"Then let her think you're weird, as long as you're genuinely doing what you think is right—and you're doing it because it *is* right, not just because you want to make a splash." She nodded at the heaping plate the waitress was putting in front of Lily. "Speaking of 'splash,'" she said, "there's enough gravy on that plate to take a bath in."

"I *love* gravy on my potatoes," Lily said.

Mom's mouth twitched. "That's my girl," she said.

They "pigged out," as Mom put it, and then took a walk around old Burlington. They scuffed through the leaves and stopped in at the practically ancient St. Mary's Church to listen to the bells and say some prayers for Reni. As they sat there, side-by-side, Lily got a different kind of prickle. It was a tingle, reminding her how cool Mom was. *I don't have to wait 'til I'm twenty-five,* Lily thought. *I think she's way smart already.*

On Monday Lily had a chance to test out her mom's wisdom. She was walking into first period when she ran into Bernadette, who was blocking the doorway. To Lily's surprise, she said, "Come here, Lily— I need your help."

Really? Lily wanted to say to her. *I thought I was too weird for you.*

But she could almost hear Mom's voice in her head, and she smiled at Bernadette. "What do you need?" she said.

Bernadette pulled Lily across the hall, looking her up and down as she dragged her along.

"I have to tell you," Bernadette said, "I'm glad you aren't wearing one of those T-shirts today. That isn't a good look for you."

The words sounded so false coming out of Bernadette's mouth. Lily was sure she was quoting them from some TV show or something.

Bernadette was now scanning the hall with her eyes.

"Who are you looking for?" Lily said.

"Benjamin. He should be coming back from the office. That stupid police person hauled him in this morning just because he was calling Shad Shifferdecker a moron."

"Shad Shifferdecker *is* a moron," Lily said. "What was the big deal?"

Bernadette flung a hand carelessly in the air. "Oh, Benjamin was kind of cussing at Shad. She got all huffy about it and made him go with her to the office. It's so stupid. We should be allowed to say whatever we want when we're not in class." She tugged playfully at Lily's backpack strap. "You protest stuff all the time. Can't you and that foreigner girl do something? I mean, you don't have to make T-shirts, I mean, definitely *don't*, but—"

Lily pulled her backpack away from Bernadette's hand and shook her head. "I only stand up for causes that are worth fighting for, and this one's not. I don't want to hear a bunch of kids swearing in the halls either—even if it *is* at Shad Shifferdecker."

"Whatever!" Bernadette said. "You are so weird—"

"Yeah," Lily said—and headed to class.

There was another person Lily wanted to settle things with, and that was Mr. Miniver. It wasn't her day to see him, and she was trying to figure out a way to fit it in when Ms. Bavetta dropped a note from the office on her desk.

"See me next period," Mr. Miniver had written. "Important!"

He's writing Girlz-Gramz now, Lily thought.

That was the best part of what was happening right now—having the Girlz back. They'd been meeting every afternoon at Zooey's—and even though Zooey's mom got teary-eyed every time, it was a way-beyond-happy time. They all talked at once, catching each other up on every detail of their lives since they'd split up and planning a sleepover for Friday night.

Yeah, Lily thought. *That's the best.*

And yet, it wasn't. What happened second period was the best. It was *the* best—no contest.

Chapter 14

When Lily got to Mr. Miniver's office, he wasn't alone. Mr. Lamb was there. So was a woman Lily had never seen before. The woman obviously didn't work at the middle school because she was wearing a suit. And Dad was there too. Lily's heart started to pound.

"No need to be nervous," the woman said. "I don't bite."

She smiled out of a perfectly made-up face and sounded pleasant enough, but Lily still sat next to Dad and got as close to him as she could. If he had torn himself away from teaching college students about medieval literature, this was serious.

"Lily," Mr. Miniver said, "this is Mrs. Morse. She's the music coordinator for Burlington County Schools."

"Hi," Lily said. "Is this about Reni?"

Mrs. Morse smiled again. "I can see you like to get right to the point. All right—let's do that. I am looking into this matter of possible discrimination against your friend. I'd like to ask you a few questions."

"Sure," Lily said. "Only—" She looked at her father. "Is it okay for me to talk, Dad?"

"Now is the time," he said, squeezing her hand.

"Now, Mr. Miniver and your father have assured me that there is no need for me to remind you that the accusation you've made is very serious," Mrs. Morse said.

"No," Lily said. "I already know that."

"Good—then suppose you share with me what you heard."

Lily did. With Dad holding onto her hand, she wasn't even tempted to jazz the story up here and there. She knew as she talked that it sounded genuine coming out of her mouth.

"Now I'm going to share something with you, Lily," Mrs. Morse said when she was finished, "because you've been brave enough to come forward. Since my little investigation started, three other people have come to me with similar complaints about the All-State auditions. I won't go into detail, except to say that two Puerto Rican children and a Native American, all at other schools, have been excluded as well. It now only remains for the other judges to concur, and I think we'll have a clear case of discrimination."

"Does that mean Reni will get to be in All-State?"

"That will be up to a new panel of judges to decide," Mrs. Morse said. "But I will say this—if she deserves to be in it, I will see to it that she is."

"Oh, she does," Lily said. "She's, like, so talented, and she practices all the time, and she has all this self-discipline. You don't make A's in Mrs. Reinhold's class without self-discipline!"

"Now that is so interesting," Mrs. Morse said, pulling Mr. Miniver and Dad in with a grown-up look. "You are the first witness who has not asked me right off the bat whether you will have to appear in court—which I doubt, by the way. We don't usually let these things get that far. One student asked whether there was a reward!"

"I don't want a reward," Lily said. "I'll just do whatever I have to for Reni. Plus—this just plain isn't right."

"No, it isn't. Your friend has a fine advocate in you. Dad—you should be proud."

"Oh, I am," Dad said.

Yeah, this was definitely the best, Lily decided.

It was several more days before they heard anything from Mrs. Morse. Meanwhile, Mr. Miniver and Lily became friends again, and he gave her some good advice about how to fix her reputation.

"A bad rep takes a while to change in people's minds," Mr. Miniver told her, "which is why it's always a good idea to take care of a good one in the first place. Now—if this all turns out for Reni, you'll have that in your favor."

"Oh, no," Lily said. "I don't mean to interrupt, but see, I'm not gonna tell anybody I was the one."

Mr. Miniver's mustache slowly took an upward turn, something she hadn't seen it do in a while. "You know something, Lily-Pad?" he said.

"What?" Lily said.

"I don't think you need to worry about that reputation of yours. I think it's going to take care of itself just fine."

Lily held on to that as she cringed under Mr. Nutting's sarcastic remarks, winced when Ms. Bavetta ignored her, and searched Mrs. Reinhold's face for signs of approval. It was hard, being somebody who was always being looked at with suspicion. But when it got its hardest, she remembered she had an advocate. It helped to talk to him.

It *didn't* help that the office called Lily and Reni out of Mrs. Reinhold's class right in the middle of an oral grammar drill that Friday morning. Mrs. Reinhold glared so hard at the poor little office aide, Lily thought her eyes would come right through her glasses.

Lily and Reni clung to each other as they hurried down the hall toward the office.

"It has to be about the All-State thing," Lily said.

"Do you think they're gonna tell us we have to have a trial?" Reni asked. She stopped dead at the top of the stairs. "What if you have to testify in front of a judge and everything, Lily?"

"Then I will," Lily said. But no images of courtrooms and suits like Mrs. Morse's came to Lily's mind. She just hung on to Reni's hand and pulled her down the hall to the office.

There was a crowd in Mr. Miniver's conference room—Reni's Mom and Dad, Mr. Miniver, Mrs. Morse, Mr. Lamb, and two women who looked vaguely familiar to Lily. The way Reni tightened her grip on Lily's hand, she was pretty certain they were the other two judges she'd seen in the orchestra room.

Mrs. Morse wasn't smiling, which worried Lily. But she tried to keep her heart from hammering its way right out of her chest as she sat down in the seat Mr. Miniver had saved for her.

"We have finally reached a resolution on this matter of the All-State audition," Mrs. Morse said. "I just want you to know—all of you—that I am extremely saddened by the result."

By now, Reni was nearly cutting off Lily's circulation. *Pray,* Lily said with her eyes. *Pray hard!*

Mrs. Morse nodded sharply at the two women sitting to her left. "There are two people here who have something to say to you."

Lily didn't dare let herself think. She just watched.

"Is this the girl?" one of the women said, pointing at Lily.

Mrs. Morse nodded, again sharply.

The woman leveled a green-eyed gaze at Lily. "You thought you heard something in that hallway."

"I did hear it," Lily said. She could barely breathe, but she kept her eyes hooked onto the woman's.

The woman, however, couldn't keep looking at Lily. Her gaze fell. "I heard it too," she said.

"So did I," said the other woman. "And—is it Reni?"

Reni was apparently having some respiratory problems herself, because she just nodded.

"Reni, we owe you an apology. We allowed someone else with seniority and a domineering attitude to sway us. We never should have done that. You should have been admitted to the All-State Orchestra on the spot."

"And you will be, Reni," Mrs. Morse said.

"Definitely," the first woman said. "And again, we apologize."

"What about the other judge?" Reni's dad said. "Doesn't my daughter get an apology from him?"

"I thought it wise not to invite him to this meeting," Mrs. Morse said. She straightened the lapels on her suit, as if she were suddenly uncomfortable. "We are dealing with a dyed-in-the-wool bigot, Mr. Johnson. I could not be confident that he wouldn't let some racial slur slip out while we were all gathered here. I felt Reni had suffered enough."

Mr. Johnson nodded, and Mrs. Morse turned to Reni. "Is there anything you'd like to say?"

"No," Reni said, "except thank you. I wanted this more than anything."

"That's the spirit we want to see in our program," Mrs. Morse said. "What about you, Lily?"

Lily saw a gleam come into Mr. Miniver's eyes. *You don't need to give a speech, Lily-Pad,* she could feel him telling her.

She didn't have to be reminded. She looked at the second woman. "I know how it is when you have to deal with attitudes," she said. "Sometimes it takes a while to figure it out."

The only person in the room who seemed to understand what she was talking about was Mr. Miniver. The mustache was practically doing the polka.

He dismissed Lily, although they kept Reni to go over some details about All-State. As Lily headed back for Mrs. Reinhold's room, she knew her own mustache would be doing some kind of dance if she had one. She felt light and clear.

It wasn't at all like the smug way she'd felt after winning the dispute with Ms. Bavetta over Benjamin and Bernadette's seats or even like the victorious feeling she'd had when she and Kresha had "shown" Mr. Nutting they hadn't been cheating.

Wow, she thought. Her steps slowed. *This is like—a God-feeling!*

She stopped completely and sat down on the first horizontal surface she could find.

Is that you, God? she prayed. *Talking to me for real? Telling me I did good?*

She squeezed her eyes shut tighter. *You did good too, God. Matter of fact, you did it* all—

"What's going on, Robbins?"

Lily's eyes flew open. The second she realized Officer Horn was standing in front of her, she sprang up. Her stomach churned as she realized she'd been sitting on *the* bench.

"I'm sorry," Lily said. "I have a pass—I was in the office—I should have gone straight back to class but—"

"Sit down, Robbins," Officer Horn said. "I want to talk to you."

Lily sank to the bench and moaned silently. This had been such a good day too.

Officer Horn sat down beside her. Lily stared. She had never seen the woman sit before.

"I've been watching you, Robbins," she said.

"I know. You told me you would—and that's okay—I know I did it to myself—"

"Can you just shut up for five seconds? I never knew a kid who could talk a blue streak the way you can."

"I do that," Lily said.

"Yeah, well, stop doing it so I can get a word in."

Lily nodded.

"You've stopped trying to push my buttons," she said. "What's going on?"

"I found out that wasn't the way to get things done," Lily said. "I shouldn't have disrespected you and tried to push things. I'm not doing that anymore, even if I do think certain rules aren't fair. I have to get my reputation back before I start trying to change things."

"So what rules aren't fair?" Officer Horn asked.

Lily carefully studied the toes of her sneakers. "Well, no offense, but I don't think it's fair that my friends and I can't hang out together before school. I know we were out of line that day—but they're not like that, really. It was all my fault and—"

"Stop right there," Officer Horn said. "You don't have to say another word. I've heard what I wanted to hear."

Lily tried to let it go—but she had to ask. "What did you hear?" she said.

Officer Horn then did the most amazing thing that happened that whole day. She slung her arm around Lily's shoulder and laughed. She actually laughed.

"You are a piece of work, Robbins," she said. "I just heard you take responsibility for your actions. If every kid in this school could do that, my job would be a piece of cake. No—I wouldn't even have a job."

"Oh," Lily said. "Then I won't spread it around."

"Don't worry about it, Robbins," Officer Horn said. "Most kids wouldn't get it if you branded it on them." She shook her head at Lily. "No, girlfriend—you're not like any other kid I ever met." She stood up, hooked her thumbs into her belt, and put on her officer face again. "Now—get to class. And tomorrow morning I want to see you."

"You do?"

"Yes, I do. Right here—on this bench—with your little pack of friends." She turned to walk away. "And make sure you have enough food for me."

Lily grinned all the way to class. It was going to be the perfect way to celebrate. Just wait 'til she told her Girlz.

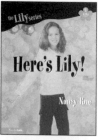

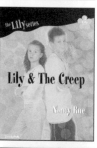

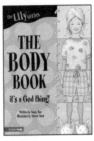

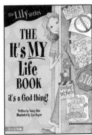

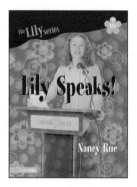

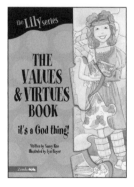

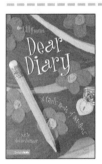